# VENGEFUL JUSTICE

## THE COWBOY JUSTICE ASSOCIATION
## BOOK NINE

# By Olivia Jaymes

www.OliviaJaymes.com

# Vengeful Justice

**Cowboy Command was only the beginning... follow along as Olivia Jaymes revisits the first couple of the Cowboy Justice series.**

Sheriff Seth Reilly and his beautiful wife Presley have a terrific life – two fantastic children, good friends, and lots and lots of love. Of course nothing worthwhile is ever easy and that's true for them too. Between their busy careers and the needs of their family, it's hard to find quality time together. More nights than not, there's a toddler, a snoring dog, and at least two stuffed animals sleeping between them in bed.

It's all pretty boring and routine until the day Seth gets the news that a man he put behind bars has been paroled and is looking for revenge. Seth took what he most loved in the world and now the escapee is going to return the favor. For the second time in her life, someone wants Presley dead and this time the stakes are even higher.

Because Presley isn't just the woman Seth loves, she's his whole world.

# Chapter One

All Sheriff Seth Reilly wanted was an ice cold beer, his recliner, and a kiss from his beautiful wife Presley. It had been a long day of dealing with people – a few calm and easygoing but most pissed off and ornery. Seth generally didn't see people on the best day of their lives and that meant that his days were filled with anger, angst, and even tears.

It didn't help that the weather was unseasonably hot and he'd sweated through a white t-shirt and his beige cotton uniform button-down. The heat also seemed to have an effect on the folks in Harper and the most even-tempered residents had turned into irritable demons. By six o'clock he'd had quite enough of his fellow human beings and was ready to be welcomed back into the bosom of his family.

"Honey, I'm home," he called as he stomped in the front door and kicked off his heavy boots. "And I'm starving."

The living room looked like a toy tornado had hit it. Blocks scattered across the floor threatening to break an ankle. Train parts strewn on the coffee table. Action figures mingled with a herd of teddy bears who lay face down on the carpet as if victims in a horrible bear homicide. Seth had to fight the urge to wrap bright yellow crime scene tape around the room. He had a roll in the SUV but perhaps he needed to store it in the house.

Instead of a warm armful of woman greeting him at the door with a smile, Seth heard a screech from the general direction of the kitchen and hurried to see if anyone had been hurt. He found Presley trying to wrestle their two-year-old Lulu out of the pan cabinet while their oldest, Ben, chased their black Labrador Fergus around the kitchen in circles.

"Bennett Elvis Reilly, stop that this minute," Presley said firmly. "Or you will sit on the naughty step. Lorelei Priscilla, please let go of Mommy's frying pan."

His wife managed to extricate the handle of the pan from the toddler's death grip but Lulu, who was in full tilt toddler mode these days, decided that now was a dandy time to throw a tantrum. The scream she let out made the screech he'd heard earlier sound positively melodious. Then she hurtled her tiny little body to the ground and proceeded to cry while pounded her fists against the tile. It was a new experience, as Ben hadn't been the tantrum type.

It was at this point that Presley appeared to notice he'd arrived home, and her expression turned to one of relief. "I'm so glad you're home."

Seth had to speak loudly to be heard over the sobbing, but he stepped forward to wrap his arms around his wife. He didn't get that far. "Me too, hon—"

"Can get your son to stop terrorizing the dog and then please get the clothes out of the dryer before they wrinkle? Thanks."

Presley was trying to take care of their two children all while starting her own business. She and Eliza were opening the first coffee shop in Harper and she'd been working some long hours to get it set up. She was probably exhausted and he hadn't been much help lately since they'd had a rash of deputies out with the flu. However, his guys were all back to one hundred percent so from now on he was going to be pulling his weight around here. He'd been relying on Presley way too much and she needed a back rub.

His fingers massaged the tight muscles of her shoulders as they were serenaded by Lulu's bellows of injustice. "Rough day?"

Slumping against the stove, Presley groaned. "You have no idea. I'm sorry I didn't say hello. I am glad you're home and not just because of the laundry."

"I'm on it, honey. Super Seth to the rescue." He looked down to the floor where Lulu was winding up her tantrum. "Are we still ignoring her when she does this or are we intervening?"

"The other moms say that giving her any attention is only rewarding the behavior. They are obviously stronger people than I am."

Lulu had finished screaming and crying and she was now trying to get another pan from the open cabinet. Seth scooped her up into his arms and give her a big kiss on her cheek.

"How's my ladybug?"

Lulu replied but only a few of the words were recognizable due to the sniffles from her earlier sobs.

Dog. Cookie. Kiss.

So Seth gave her another kiss on the other cheek.

"No cookies, ladybug. We're going to have dinner in a few minutes."

Ben had finally finished chasing Fergus around the house and had paused in the kitchen, deciding to give his father some attention. Finally. He used to run to meet Seth at the door but now toys and cartoons were more important.

"She had two cookies earlier at the coffee shop," Ben said. "Mom gave them to her."

Seth's son was in the tattling stage and he didn't care who he told on. He'd told Presley that Seth had snuck a beer while working on the deck. He'd told Seth's mother that Presley said a bad word while driving. He'd told them Fergus had stolen a sandwich right off the kitchen counter. But Lulu was his favorite person to tell on.

"If your mother gave her cookies, then it's okay," Seth sighed. "Come here and give your old man a hug and then tell me what you did today."

Ben glommed onto Seth's leg and didn't let go which made grabbing the laundry a challenge. With Lulu sitting on the top of the dryer and Ben hanging off of his thigh the two kids chattered away about their day. Highlights included cookies, Grandma, Aunt Eliza, and seeing a deer.

"Sounds like you had a big day, but we need to get you fed and in the tub. It's going to be your bedtime soon."

The kids wound down as the evening progressed. Somehow they all four managed to eat dinner without any major catastrophes and he gave the kids their bath while Presley cleaned up the kitchen. He'd offered to do the dishes but she'd just smiled and said this was his time with Ben and Lulu.

This was Seth's favorite time of day.

After making sure the kids were squeaky clean, he lounged in the bathroom while Ben and Lulu played in the water, splashing and giggling. At some point, Presley would poke her head in and see if he needed any help but he enjoyed getting them into their jammies and tucking them into bed. It was his night to read them a story and Lulu chose a book about naughty dinosaurs who didn't listen to their human parents. Presley joined them and read a second book about a bunny who misbehaved too. There was a theme among these books.

The usual hugs and kisses concluded and then Seth turned

4

out the lights with an exhausted sigh. He loved his children but they could really kick his ass.

Presley elbowed him gently in the ribs. "Why don't you go take a shower and I'll get you a beer?"

Seth leaned down and pressed a long kiss to his wife's full lips. "I'll take that deal all day long, baby. Thank you."

"It's just one of the many services we offer here, Sheriff."

There was promise in that tone. Seth was a lucky man to have a woman like Presley and he tried to never take her for granted.

"Don't be too long," he said as she bounded down the stairs. He turned and headed into the master bedroom only to groan at the sight before him. Fergus was lying on the bed with a guilty look on his face and it was easy to see why. He'd dragged all of the trash out of the bathroom garbage can and taken the time to shred every single tissue. Luckily it had been trash day this morning so there hadn't been much in it to begin with.

"Bad dog," Seth said to the reclining Labrador who just whined in response. "Very bad dog."

Picking up the trail of tissues that led into the bathroom, Seth stopped short when he saw another item that had been dragged out of the trash can. Gingerly picking up the plastic stick, Seth's heart stopped beating in his chest for a long moment before kickstarting painfully direct to a gallop. It couldn't be. But there it was. He couldn't deny what was in in his own hand and in front of his own two eyes.

A pregnancy test.

A *positive* pregnancy test.

Presley was pregnant.

As in a baby. They were going to have another child.

Sitting down on the cold tile, he stared at the plus sign on the test. He didn't need to check the directions on the box. This wasn't the first time he'd seen this and he knew what it meant.

*We weren't going to have any more children.*

About a year after weaning Lulu off the bottle they'd sat down and talked it out. The pros and cons of a third child and they'd both agreed. No more kids. He'd even agreed to get a vasectomy, except that he hadn't quite got around to it all this time later. He'd kept putting it off and making excuses, despite his physician's assurances that it was a simple procedure. Snip, snip.

The pill made Presley nauseous so they'd been using condoms. They were pretty good about it but there were times...

A baby.

Was Presley happy about it? She'd had problems with her pregnancy with Lulu and had to be put on bedrest. Here she was in the middle of opening up her coffee shop and now a baby on top of it. This was her dream and dammit, Seth wanted her to have it. But he also couldn't help but think about how it might be to have another baby in the house. Another little body to cuddle. That amazing baby smell. Sure, there were sleepless nights and spit up, dirty diapers and colic, but there was so much love too. Another baby that was a product of his adoration for Presley.

A smile curved his lips as he tucked everything back into the trash can. They were going to have a baby and Seth was thrilled. Already he was wondering if it was a boy or a girl. Would it favor him or Presley?

The better question was when she was planning to tell him the big news? Seth could simply wait for her to come to bed and then tell her he had found the test stick but it would be more fun to wait and see how she did it. With Ben she'd made a game out of it and then with Lulu she'd taken him on a special weekend trip to Denver, just the two of them. Knowing Presley, she was already planning on how she would tell him and he didn't want to ruin it for her. He'd wait even if it killed him.

They were having another baby.

# CHAPTER TWO

The next day Presley and her friend and business partner Eliza painted the walls of the main room in their new coffee house. With any luck, they'd be open in about a month. Worst case scenario, sixty days. There was still some carpentry that needed done, plus they were waiting on delivery of some of the equipment but it was slowly all coming together. She and Eliza were going to be business owners. It was a dream come true. Finally she was doing something more with her life than drifting from job to job with no real direction.

*I have an amazing husband, two great kids, and now a coffee shop.*

"I'm just saying it was weird," Presley said to Eliza as they worked alongside each other. Eliza had paint in her dark hair and Presley's shirt was covered in speckles. "Seth was acting very strange last night after we put the kids to bed. He kept smiling and humming. It was a little creepy."

Eliza dipped her roller into the paint tray. "Wait a minute. Seth always looks happy around you."

"This was different. It was…heck, I don't know. It was like he was trying too hard, acting over the top. There was nothing out of the ordinary going on last night. We ate dinner, put the kids to bed, watched some television. But he was grinning like the Joker in one of Ben's Batman cartoons."

"That is creepy. Maybe he has some sort of surprise for you. Isn't your birthday coming up?"

Presley snorted. "In a month. Since when has Seth Reilly planned a birthday celebration a full thirty days ahead? No, this is something else."

"I think the paint fumes have made you paranoid," Eliza laughed. "Your husband is happy and that makes you suspicious."

Putting down the paint roller, Presley wiped her hands on an old rag before taking a sip from her water bottle. "Lately he's been talking about how one of his deputies just bought a motorcycle and I could tell he was jealous. Maybe Seth spent our vacation money on a Harley and he's afraid to tell me."

"That would make him scared, not happy," Eliza pointed out. "Unless he's trying to cover up his fear that you'll kill him."

"I'm not sure I'd go that far but I would be surprised that he did it."

Eliza put down her own roller and rubbed at her shoulders. "I'm sure it's nothing that you'll need to commit homicide over. I still think it might be something about your birthday. What did he do last year?"

Presley thought back to her last birthday and sighed. "We'd planned to go to Seattle for a long weekend but both Ben and Lulu got the stomach flu. Then of course Seth came down with it too. There wasn't much celebrating going on for about a week."

Eliza's brows pinched together. "That's terrible. But eventually you all got better, right?"

They had and Seth had tried to make it up to her but there just didn't seem to be any time for just the two of them anymore. She wouldn't trade her children for anything in the world though. She adored them with all of her being.

But just once she'd like to go to the bathroom by herself.

"We did recover and Seth brought home a birthday cake a few weeks later when we could all face food again."

"So maybe he's trying to make up for last year by planning something big this year. Something amazing…like Vegas."

Sitting down on one of the metal folding chairs, Presley stretched out her tired legs. Every now and then she and Seth would sit around and dream about running away for a long weekend and Vegas would always be one of the places they wanted to visit. "I would love to go to Vegas but I doubt that's going to happen."

"Name two reasons why it couldn't happen," Eliza challenged, plopping into another chair across from Presley.

Two reasons? The truth was cruel.

Presley held up one finger. "One. Money. We've spent so much on the coffee shop there is no way that Seth would take me to Vegas. You know how cautious he is and hell, I've become just like him lately. Sure, we could absolutely afford to go but then we'd sit around and think of all the other uses that money would be. New kitchen cabinets. Snow tires. College funds. All the boring crap adults have to think about."

"That's one. What's the second?"

The second was the worst. No more spontaneity. She had to be super organized to be able to get everything done every day that needed to be done.

Presley held up another finger. "And two? This one sucks. We're not exciting anymore. We don't do things on the spur of the moment. We plan and think things through. We only do things that make sense. We're boring and stuck in a rut. No wait. I'm boring. I'm not exciting anymore. Seth is the way he's always been. It's me that's changed and that's probably the crux of all of this. He has to force himself to pretend he's happy when he's bored out of his gourd. He's probably been trying not to fall asleep for a couple of years now."

Eliza wore a scandalized expression. "There is no way that is true. Seth worships the ground you walk on, girl. You are not boring."

Quirking an eyebrow, Presley almost choked on a gulp of water. "Really? Be honest. Am I the same person you met that first day in the diner?"

"Well…no," Eliza conceded, her cheeks turning pink. "Of course everyone changes. But there's a great deal about you that's the same. That's why we're opening this coffee shop. People gravitate toward you. You make them feel welcome and at home wherever you are. That's a wonderful quality to have."

Presley leaned forward in her chair. "But am I exciting any-more?"

Eliza threw up her hands. "Define exciting."

"I'll take that as a no." Presley slapped her forehead and groaned. "What am I doing? We shouldn't be talking about me and my problems. We should be talking about you. You and your wonderful news. Did you tell Alex last night that you're pregnant?"

Eliza had shown up at Presley's door yesterday afternoon, nervous and almost in tears. After two years of infertility, she was late. Very late and she wanted to take a pregnancy test but she was scared after all the negative tests and all the disappoint-ment. Presley had ushered her friend in and had been supportive while Eliza peed on three test sticks on the other side of the door. They'd all been positive and Presley was thrilled for her friend.

"I did and I don't think I've ever seen him that happy," Eliza sighed blissfully, then smiled and waggled her brows. "Needless to say, we celebrated."

"That's what got you in this situation in the first place."

"Lucky me." Eliza giggled but then turned serious. "Listen, why don't you bring the kids over to my house on Friday night? Alex and I will watch them for the weekend and you and Seth can have some lovey-dovey couple time."

"I couldn't ask you to—"

Eliza waved Presley's objections away. "I insist. We could use the parenting practice. What do you say?"

Time with Seth? Presley would never say no to that. Maybe it wouldn't be so bad for Eliza and Alex. Ben and Lulu often behaved better for other people than they did for Mom and Dad.

"I say yes and a huge thank you."

She was already making plans. Not so boring plans. Lingerie. Champagne. Maybe even some candlelight. Forty-eight hours to make love to her husband. She wouldn't waste a minute of it.

The next morning, Deputy Hank stood next to Seth's desk, a grim expression on his face.

"You got a minute? It's important."

Seth hadn't even finished his first cup of coffee, made by Presley at home and poured lovingly into a to-go cup so he wouldn't miss a drop of the delicious brew, but his senior deputy didn't normally look like his dog had died.

"Sure, have a seat."

The sheriff's station didn't have much privacy but they were the only two there except for Nina, the new administrative assistant, and she had earbuds in listening to music. Seth doubted that even if she could hear them speaking, she wouldn't care to listen.

Settling into the chair across from Seth, Hank seemed to struggle with what to say.

"There's been news and I'm going to tell you but I don't want you to overreact."

Carefully placing his cup on the desk, Seth nodded calmly. "You know those sorts of statements are exactly the kind that get people to overreact, right? Just saying *don't overreact* can make people, in fact, overreact when they might not have otherwise."

Hank winced. "Jesus, you sound like my wife."

That made Seth chuckle. "Alyssa is a wise woman. Now what am I supposed to not get upset about? Are they trying to get me to run for mayor again because that shit is definitely not happening. That's a thankless fucking job if I ever saw one."

"No, the governor's office called."

"They want me to run for governor? Now that sounds a hell of a lot better, although the governor's mansion is a bit small for my taste."

Seth had been teasing but apparently this was no happy situation. Hank leaned forward, his lips a thin line. "You need to listen to me. The governor's office called."

Seth shut up this time and waited for the second part of the statement. He didn't have to wait long.

"About Danny Harbaugh."

Hank now had Seth's complete and undivided attention. Danny Harbaugh was serving time for an attempted bank heist with his wife. A teller had been shot and killed along with Danny's wife Lyndsey in the ensuing firefight.

"He still threatening revenge on me when he gets out?"

"Hard to say since Harbaugh was paroled day before yesterday but if I were to hazard a guess I'd say yes."

Surely Seth hadn't heard his deputy correctly. "Paroled?

What the fuck are you talking about? There is no way Harbaugh could be paroled."

"This is why I warned you not to get upset," Hank said, exhaling noisily. "You need to keep a cool head on your shoulders with this guy on the outside."

But Seth was still in denial. "I'm not following you at all. How on earth did he get parole? It's insane. And how are we just finding out about this now?"

"He's been a model fucking prisoner from all reports. He took classes and now has a certificate in airplane mechanics. He counseled new arrivals to help them transition."

"Sounds like he's been a ray of sunshine in that place," Seth snarked. "And it's all an act. He's a goddamn narcissistic sociopath. You cannot reform a person like that."

"You know how it is...budget cuts and pressure to lower prison population. He looked all shiny and new to the parole board. A reform story they can brag about, and they needed one after that other guy got out and slaughtered a family a few months ago."

Seth still couldn't wrap his head around it. Harbaugh had been quite vocal at his trial when he'd been dragged away. The minute he got out he was coming for Seth as retribution for Lyndsey's death.

"To get parole a person normally has to take responsibility for their actions. I can't see Harbaugh doing that."

Hank sighed and shook his head. "I don't know if he did or not. I asked the governor's office to send us a transcript of the hearing and they said they would by email."

A little light reading to make Seth's day. Did that parole board even ask Harbaugh any questions or did they give him a Get Out of Jail Free card? Were they aware that Danny had a vendetta against a local sheriff? Obviously they had to be if the governor's office saw fit to call this morning.

"Let me know when that transcript comes in," Seth replied instead of asking all of the questions running through his head. Hank would only be frustrated that he didn't have the answers. "I think I need to make a few calls."

Seth could use some advice. And help, too.

Hank nodded and turned to go but then stopped. "Are you worried? He could be on his way here right now. Is there anything the guys need to do to keep you safe?"

"Just keep your eye out for Harbaugh and if you see him call for backup. Do not engage with him. He's dangerous and not scared, a terrible combination."

"So you're not worried?"

Laughing, Seth smiled at Hank's question. "You know the answer as well as I do. We're lawmen and that means that every damn day somebody hates our guts and wants us dead. The only difference with Danny Harbaugh is that we know he'll do it but honestly, anyone we come into contact could suddenly pull out a gun and shoot us. Every traffic stop, every domestic call, every unknown situation could be our last. Am I worried? For myself, no. For others around me, yes. I don't need anyone hurt or killed in the crossfire."

And that meant Presley and the kids. He'd do whatever it took to keep them safe.

# CHAPTER THREE

The roadhouse Seth and his sheriff-friends usually met at one Sunday each month was open during the week so they had to find somewhere else. The group ended up in Griffin Sawyer's tiny town sitting on metal folding chairs on the stage of the local theatre. Griffin's wife Jazz, herself a former actress in Hollywood, had opened the venue a while back and held acting and music classes as well as local productions utilizing not only adults, but children too.

Griffin flipped open a small cooler filled with ice and sodas. "Since I'm the host today this was all I was able to put together at the last minute. Sorry it's not more. Jazz says we have the place for two hours, by the way."

That would be plenty of time. This wasn't a regular meeting, but rather one that Seth had called for a specific reason.

For years now, these lawmen had been meeting on a regular basis to share information and help one another out. Although they ran separate towns, their issues and problems were often similar and sometimes connected. They'd become exponentially more effective at their jobs since they'd decided to work together. Seth didn't quite remember how it all got started. He'd known Tanner Marks for a long time and had played football against Reed but the details of the decision to start meeting were fuzzy. He only knew that these were some of the best friends he had in the world and he would trust them with his life.

He would trust them with Presley, Ben, and Lulu's life. That was saying something.

"I'd like to thank everyone for coming on such short notice," Seth said to open the meeting. "I know you all are busy and had other activities planned today but this is important and could affect not just myself, but all of us. I got word early this morning that Danny Harbaugh was paroled from prison."

The group erupted, all the men talking loudly at once, the sound bouncing off the walls of the auditorium. Seth tried to get their attention so he could continue speaking but had to resort to an ear-piercing whistle to get them to finally stop talking.

"I get it," he said when they'd quieted down. "I'm not happy about it either. Harbaugh is trouble and we all know that. Even if he didn't threaten me, he'd be up to no good on the outside. We all need to be vigilant because I have no doubt he has something planned besides putting me six feet under."

Three worried expressions – and one scowl – stared back at Seth. Tanner Marks was the oldest and most experienced lawman and the unofficial leader of the group. Griffin Sawyer, Reed Mitchell, and Dare Turner – the one who was scowling – were all about Seth's age and level of experience.

"We need a plan," Tanner stated, his gaze roaming around the circle. "We don't want to be caught with our pants down, so to speak."

Reed nodded in agreement. "We do but I don't like the idea of sitting around waiting for this douchebag to come at us. How can we go get him?"

"He has to do something first," Griffin replied, tapping his chin in thought. "Has he reported in to his parole officer yet? We need to talk to him or her."

Dare was an ornery son of a bitch, although more mellow since marrying Rayne, a local tattoo artist, but he currently looked as unhappy as Seth could remember. "That's not why Seth called us here."

Yes and no. It was part of why Seth had asked to meet but the more important reason he hadn't spoken about yet.

Sighing, Tanner nodded. "Presley and the kids. Jesus, you don't think he'd come after them, do you?"

"Seth calls Harbaugh a sociopath," Dare retorted. "I just think he's plumb insane. He'd go after them or the President of the whole United States if he thought that's what he needed to do."

Seth had replayed that shootout in the alley over and over a million times in his head and he still hadn't figured out how he'd shot Lyndsey Harbaugh. He hadn't been aiming in her direction but she'd shot out from behind their vehicle, trying to take closer cover behind a garbage can. Needless to say, she hadn't made it and Danny had been livid.

"Yes, I'm concerned about him going after my family," Seth stated. "I don't worry for myself but Danny's not playing by society's rules anymore. My guess is he feels like he has nothing to lose."

"And completely convinced he's in the right," Reed added. "He has a cause, whereas before he was just a thug. Now he's a thug on a mission."

"The most dangerous kind," Griffin said grimly.

"So we need to figure out how to handle someone who is unpredictable, erratic, and zealot-like in their decision making," Tanner said, bringing the group back around as he always did. "We need to put together a plan to protect Seth's family and then also a way to be a shitload more proactive in this situation. Like you, I hate the idea that we're sitting around on our asses waiting for this guy to hurt a few people or knock over a liquor store. Seth, we're going to need the trial transcripts. Can you get those? There might be a clue there as to where or who he might go to now that he's out."

"I've got them at the station. I also have our case file and the parole hearing paperwork from the governor's office. What I don't have is the prosecution's file."

Reed raised his hand. "I can help with that. I have friends in the county office."

"We need some deep background on Harbaugh," Dare said, pulling out his cell phone and tapping in a note. "I'll see what I can dig up with some web searches."

Griffin elbowed Dare, who only scowled in response. "Look who thinks they're Jared all of the sudden."

Jared Monroe had been another sheriff in their group until he started his own consulting firm.

"Who do you think taught Jared everything he knows?" Dare mocked, tucking his phone back into his breast pocket. "It's only the internet, dude. Don't let the ones and zeros intimidate you."

"Can we focus here?" Seth asked. "It's only the lives of my wife and kids at stake."

"Yes, we can," Tanner said, giving a warning look to Dare and Griffin. "Now let's get to work. We have some preparations to make. Looks like we'll all be pulling some unofficial overtime until this guy is back behind bars."

With any luck, it wouldn't be long.

✧ ✧ ✧ ✧

Presley's mother-in-law Marion lifted the bubbling lasagna out of the oven, the smell of tomatoes and garlic permeating the air making her mouth water. Seth and his dad George were out in the living room with the kids watching Scooby Doo cartoons and Presley wasn't sure who was enjoying it more, Ben and Lulu or the men.

"Thanks for inviting us over for dinner tonight," Presley said, setting the large table in the kitchen. It was only the six of them tonight so they didn't need the even longer table in the dining room. Seth's brothers and their wives were eating in their own homes tonight.

"It was my pleasure," Marion assured her. "George loves lasagna but we can't eat a whole pan of it on our own and even with leftovers it can go to waste."

"It won't with Seth around, and I am grateful. If you hadn't called we'd be having frozen pizza for dinner."

Marion's expression turned sympathetic. "You know all you have to do is ask for help and we'd lend a hand. Your sisters-in-law said the same when they were here for Sunday dinner."

Sarah and Cindy had offered to help but they had their hands full with their own growing broods. It didn't seem fair to ask others to spend their precious free time working at the coffee shop.

"I know but you're all so busy. Eliza and I will get it all done. We painted today and things are coming along. It's just not as fast as I'd hoped. I'm just impatient, that's all."

Bustling over to the refrigerator, Presley retrieved the pitcher of iced tea along with a jug of milk for the children and filled the glasses.

"Just know that we're here for you."

Stowing the beverages back in the refrigerator, Presley gave Marion a huge hug. "I know you are and I'm grateful. I really am. But you shouldn't be worried about me or the coffee shop. You should be thinking about your vacation. Don't you leave the day after tomorrow?"

Huge Elvis fans, it was time for George and Marion's yearly trip to Graceland. They'd only missed once in the last twenty years and that was eight years ago when George broke his leg.

"We do and I have to admit that I'm excited," Marion sighed happily. "We've made friends there that we only see during this trip, plus we have a line on a new collectible dealer that we want to meet. We'd love to add something to our collection."

Presley's in-laws had an Elvis room in their home filled to the brim with items they'd lovingly collected during their marriage. The King was much more than a hobby for George and Marion. It was a passion they both shared.

"Do you think you have the room?" Presley teased with a grin. "You may need a bigger space."

"Then I'll have George knock down a wall. He needs a good project. Since he retired and handed the ranch over to Sam and Jason, he's been underfoot constantly. I have to make up errands for him just so I can send him into town and out of my hair." Marion's eyes lit up. "Wait a minute. Why didn't I think of that before? I'll send George over to the coffee shop to help you."

If the older woman only knew. George had taken to hanging out at the coffee shop with Eliza and Presley for the same reason Marion sent him on errands. They were still getting used to all the togetherness that retirement created. It was for that reason Presley had been prodding Seth to help his dad find a hobby.

"Where do you think he goes when you send him to the hardware store or the market? He comes to the shop where I absolutely waste no time in putting him to work."

"Then I owe you one."

The family sat down to dinner and as always it was a lively meal. The Reilly clan wasn't the type to sit quietly at the table and barely speak. They talked about everything under the sun whether they agreed on it or not. In fact, Presley wasn't sure they enjoyed the topics they didn't agree on more than those they did. Nothing excited a Reilly man more than a good debate and a fine meal. It explained a hell of a lot about Seth...like how he always wanted to be right.

"Do you need help loading the minivan, Dad? I can stop by tomorrow night and give you a hand."

George Reilly lowered his chin and gave his middle son a hard stare that had Seth – a grown man – squirming in his chair. "Just because I'm retired doesn't mean I'm so feeble that I can't load two or three suitcases into the back of a van. We're not packing up the whole house, just enough to get us through a couple of weeks."

Marion smiled and patted her husband's hand. "In other words, thank you for the kind offer but we've got it. George, Seth was being a thoughtful son."

Now it was George fidgeting in his seat under the watchful eye of his loving wife. "Thank you, son, but I'll be fine."

"I wish we could take the kids to Graceland," Seth said wistfully. "They both really like Elvis. But I don't see that happening for at least another year, maybe two. You love Elvis don't you, Ben?"

Just as Presley was trying to get her oldest child's mouth wiped down, he burst into a fairly decent rendition of "Don't Be Cruel", complete with giggles and gyrations that had him almost falling out of his booster seat.

Sometimes the hardest part of being a mother was trying not to laugh when she was supposed to be an adult and in charge. She should be wiping the tomato sauce and cheese off of his cute cheeks and grubby hands but he was simply too adorable when he did his Elvis impression.

Lulu was also singing along, a little off-key but still just as sweet. She jumped off her chair and wiggled her hips like she was wearing a rhinestone studded white jumpsuit and sideburns.

*My beautiful babies.*

Marion's smile widened and she clapped her hands together. "Why don't we take them with us?"

*Wait. What? I don't think I heard that right.*

"Take them with you?" Presley repeated, unsure as to what Marion could be talking about. "I don't follow."

"They could go with us." George was grinning too, as was Seth. Apparently, she was the only one not getting thrilled. "It would be great. A trip with Grandma and Grandpa just for them—plus that would give you more time to work on the coffee shop. It's a win for everyone."

It wasn't a win for her. They were talking about taking her babies not just out of town, but to another state. Thousands of miles.

"It's a great opportunity for the kids to bond with their grandparents, honey," Seth urged. "They'll have the time of their lives."

But Presley wouldn't be there to see them have that fun. She wouldn't be tucking them in at night or getting kisses from her tiny angels.

"What if they get sick?" she finally asked, the words sticking in her throat. "Or they hurt themselves?"

"Mom raised all three of us," Seth assured her. "I'm sure she can handle Ben and Lulu."

Marion nodded in agreement. "The kids will be fine, sweetheart. We'll take good care of them. This is so exciting. Their first trip to Graceland."

As far as Presley was concerned nothing had been decided yet. She was still in the thinking about it mode. But why was Seth so all-fired up about this? Why was he pushing? Was he really so bored with her and family life that he wanted to ditch the kids for a few weeks? A night here and there made sense. Everyone needed a break but George and Marion would be gone for two weeks. Or more.

"They've never been away from us that long," Presley protested. "Just a few days here and there. This is at least two weeks, maybe longer."

George and Marion liked to take their time coming back from Graceland and often stopped along the way to see the sights and visit friends.

The smile had disappeared from George's face, replaced with a frown of concern. "I hope you know that we'd take the best care of them, Presley. Nothing is more precious to us than our grandchildren."

"I know that." Great, she'd insulted her in-laws, which was not what she'd intended. "It's just that two weeks is a long time. For them. And me."

Her gaze traveling to her two children, Presley's chest squeezed tightly as she watched Ben and Lulu giggling and laughing as they danced and sang, this time to "Blue Suede Shoes". Two whole weeks? How was she supposed to do without them all that time?

"We could do that Skype thing," Marion suggested. "Sarah has it set up on the laptop. That way you could not only talk to them, you can see each other too."

"That sounds like a terrific idea," Seth stated, a grin on his handsome face. He was definitely pushing for the children to go. "With modern technology we can keep in touch anytime and anywhere."

Presley wanted to tell her husband what he could do with his modern technology but she managed to keep her mouth shut in front of the family.

"Give me the night to think about it," she said firmly. "Is there any reason the decision has to be made right this minute?"

George and Seth looked like they wanted to argue but Marion cut them off at the pass.

"That's fine. There's no difference between deciding tonight and tomorrow morning. None at all. Now who wants pie for dessert?"

Everyone wanted pie, of course. Knowing Seth, he wanted two pieces with ice cream on top.

That was what was bothering her. Presley knew Seth...his moods, his funny affectations, his stubborn, controlling nature that he didn't much bother to hide. This Seth, however, was someone new. He wanted his children to go on a vacation for two weeks without him.

In fact, it had been his idea. He'd been the one to sort of suggest it. Even more strange.

Something was definitely going on and dammit, she was going to find out. If he was tired of being a husband and a father, if he wanted to buy a Harley and be free as a bird, he needed to nut up and just say it.

# CHAPTER FOUR

L ater that evening, Presley still wasn't sure what to think about Ben and Lulu going on vacation with her in-laws. On one hand, she absolutely trusted George and Marion. They'd take excellent care of the kids and Ben and Lulu adored their grandparents. They all spent a great deal of time together, seeing each other practically every day. But if the children happened to get homesick a thousand miles from home there wasn't an easy way to solve that problem.

Or worse…what if Ben and Lulu didn't miss their mommy at all?

Being a mother meant facing the fact that she was raising her children to leave her and become independent. She could deal with that as long as it wasn't right now. To be perfectly honest, she'd thought she'd have more time. She was still getting over Ben starting school.

Sure, it was tough having two little ones around all of the time but they wouldn't be this age forever. Soon they'd be going to prom and heading off to college, two eventualities that Presley tried not to think about much. She wanted to enjoy these years as much as possible.

However, Seth might not feel the same. Although he'd loosened up a whole bunch since he'd met her he was still a man that liked order in his life, which wasn't really possible with two small children. Maybe he wanted some quiet time and he thought this was the best way to do it. But what was next? Was he going to ship her off with his parents as well? She'd half expected him to suggest it at dinner tonight.

It was a sad day when she didn't know what was going on in her husband's head.

Maybe he simply wanted more attention from her. They hadn't exactly been...*connecting*...lately what with his job and her coffeehouse.

With renewed purpose, Presley opened up her bottom dresser drawer. It had clearly been way too long since she'd last worn this particular little number because it had migrated all the way to the bottom and she had to take everything out of the drawer to get it. Grunting with effort, she shoved all her clothes back in with a promise to organize the entire dresser situation. Just as soon as she had time.

There it was. Black silk and lace. Spaghetti straps and a low-cut neckline that just skimmed the tops of her nipples. The nightie was short, barely covering her ass but Seth had never complained. This was his favorite and they always had a very good night whenever she wore it.

Stripping out of her clothes, she tugged the negligee on and twirled in front of the bathroom mirror. Not bad for a mother of two. She wasn't some skinny girl in her twenties anymore but she'd held up pretty well. The bag boy at the grocery store still carried her purchases to her car and flirted with her. When in Florida for Evan and Josie's wedding, a man had tried to buy her a drink in the hotel bar. She still had it going on.

Hearing Seth moving around in the bedroom, Presley quickly

brushed her teeth and smoothed her hair. She didn't want him falling asleep before she could give him the attention he was so obviously missing these days. Taking a deep breath, she opened the bathroom door and stood there on display, waiting for his reaction. Lounging on the bed in just his boxers, his nose was deep in a book. All these years later just the sight of his naked chest could still do funny things to her libido. Her stomach fluttered and her heart sped up. It looked like she was going to have to remind him that she was much more interesting. And fun.

"What are you reading?"

He looked up from the book. "It's the latest— Holy hell, woman, who gives a fuck?"

Tossing it carelessly aside, Seth was sitting up on the bed and for the first time in weeks she had his undivided attention. Good.

Seth's wife was always full of surprises but this was better than most. Not once this evening had she even given him a hint that she'd had some naughty fun on her dirty little mind. He'd assumed tonight would be normal – television on in the bedroom until one of them fell asleep from sheer exhaustion. If they were lucky they'd get to sleep alone in their bed the entire night without a child or the dog crawling in between them.

"Are you surprised?" she said, a smug look on her face. "That was the plan."

Reaching for her, his fingers gripped her hips, urging her closer to the bed. His heart had already kicked into a higher gear and his cock had woken up as well. "You're a dangerous woman, Presley Reilly. You could have given me a heart attack. You're so damn sexy, and you don't need that lingerie to make you that way."

"But it doesn't hurt, does it?"

Sitting up, he pressed a kiss to the curve of her shoulder. "It does not hurt at all."

Her fingers carded through his hair as he nuzzled the valley in between her breasts, inhaling her sweet fragrance. It was light and floral and feminine and he'd never smelled a scent so wonderful on anyone else. Only Presley made him this crazy, even after all these years. She was probably going to still be turning him on when he was old and gray, telling him dirty jokes while they sat in rocking chairs on the back porch.

Stroking her satin soft skin, he slipped the thin straps of the short nightgown down, the material pooling at her waist and exposing her bare breasts to his lustful gaze. Round, full, and tipped with dusky pink nipples, they were perfection and they called to him, practically begging for his fingers and mouth. He wouldn't disappoint.

His fingers plucked at the nipple while he ran his tongue around the other, lapping at the tip until it was pebble-hard in his mouth. Her grip on his head tightened and a moan slipped from between her full lips. His own arousal surged and his cock hardened even more at the sexy sounds she was making. Presley always let him know what she liked, not leaving him to guess and wonder. Clearly he was on the right track tonight if her sighs and groans were to be believed.

Sweeping the nightie over her head, he tossed it away without a glance, content to look at his wife for a long moment, in no hurry to complete this act of love. She was his and his alone. Of course, he belonged to her as well and that was just fine with him. Currently her fingers were stroking down his spine to that place on his lower back that made him shudder with pleasure. Presley knew all his sensitive spots, just as he knew hers. For example, he knew that if he ran his tongue on the underside of her breast she'd shake in his arms.

Giggling, she turned and stretched out on the mattress while he kicked off his boxers, anxious to be free of the confining material. His cock slapped hard and ready against his stomach and he ran his hand from the base to the tip as his gaze took in Presley from the top of her head to the tip of painted toenails.

She held out her arms and beckoned him closer. Who was he to argue? "Get over here, handsome, and give your wife some sugar."

Hovering over her much smaller body, he captured her lips in a soul-searing kiss that he felt in all of his extremities. His balls were pulled tight to his body demanding satisfaction but he was determined to take his time tonight. Or as much as he could stand. He wanted Presley out of her mind with pleasure before he was done.

Trailing damp kisses over her jaw and down her neck, he paused to nip at the spot where her pulse beat madly before heading down between her breasts and over her abdomen. He dipped his tongue in her belly button, drawing another giggle from Presley who was now fisting the sheets in her hands, crumpling the linen between her white-knuckled fingers. She was going to be doing more than that quite soon.

The scent of her arousal hung heavy in the air as he pushed his shoulders between her legs, kissing and nipping a path up her inner thigh and his tongue tracing swirls on the sensitive skin. Her hips jumped under his hands and he had to hold her firmly down as he thoroughly explored every nook and cranny, especially her already swollen clit. Her legs were shaking as she hovered on the edge of her orgasm and he didn't make her wait, closing his mouth over the shiny pearl and gently sucking.

Her reaction was instantaneous and dramatic. First she

seemed to freeze, not one muscle moving, her spine completely rigid and her muscles stiff. Then her back arched off the bed and a wail escaped from between her lips as the pleasure ran through her. Her entire body shook and trembled and she rode his mouth all through her climax until she collapsed, her breathing loud and ragged in the quiet bedroom.

While she was still feeling the pleasant aftershocks, he climbed up and pressed his cock at her entrance, so drenched he slid in easily. Tight, hot, and so heavenly, it was like being wrapped in silk. Her legs went around his waist as he pulled out and thrust back in, building up speed. He knew his woman liked it hard and fast and he was going to make sure she got what she needed.

Sweat trickling down his back, he hiked her calf up so it rested on his shoulder, and then twisted his hips slightly, running the head of his cock over her G-spot. Presley's mouth fell open and she moaned his name, her voice dark and husky. It was so fucking sexy he did it over and over again – despite his own climax battering at the gate like a bucking bull that had to be let free – until he could feel her walls squeezing him with her second climax of the night. The pressure in his lower back had become too much for him and he followed her over the cliff, the heat from his orgasm so powerful he thought he might blow the top of his head off with its force.

When it was over he fell back onto the mattress, dragging her closer so her head was pillowed on his chest. They didn't say anything for a long time, simply happy that they were in each other's arms. Seth had always joked that he couldn't wait until retirement so he could have Presley in his arms every single moment of the day. Not that she'd allow that...she was far too active, always running from place to place...but this moment right now was peaceful and serene. So different from their day to day lives.

Tightening his hold around his wife, Seth made a silent vow that no one was going to get near her. No man would take Presley away from him. Ever.

# CHAPTER FIVE

L ying in Seth's arms afterward was one of Presley's favorite things in life. It was at that moment she felt so close to him, so comfortable and safe. This was their life together and she could physically feel his love, not just during but after too in the way he held her, stroked her skin, and whispered silly little things in her ear. It was then that the barriers of the day melted away and they could communicate so easily, talking about their future plans and dreams. Seth was open with her in a way that she'd never dreamed was possible.

Nestled in the crook of his arm, she rested her head on his shoulder while her fingers idly traced patterns on his chest. His heart thudded steadily under her hand, strong and sure. Just like the man lying next to her.

"I'm going to get a glass of water."

Before she could protest, he was sliding out of the bed and leaving her to enjoy the afterglow all alone.

She pointed to the water bottle by the side of the bed. Seth was a stickler for keeping one there at all times. He was all about hydration. "We have water."

Rubbing his chin, he shrugged into the Star Wars robe the

kids had picked out for his Christmas present. He rarely wore it. "I want cold water. Can I bring you anything?"

*This.* This was why she was beginning to think her husband had been replaced by a lookalike. Seth hated that robe and he didn't care what temperature his water was.

"I'm good." She patted the bed next to her. "Can't you come back and cuddle a little longer?"

He was already backing toward the bedroom door. "Thirsty but I'll be right back and we'll pick up where we left off. I promise. Love you."

Practically turning and fleeing, Seth scurried out of the bedroom and down the hallway. Something was definitely going on and she was going to find out what it was.

Throwing on one of Seth's old t-shirts, she snuck quietly as possible down the hall and peered around the doorway to the kitchen only to find the room empty. Flummoxed as to where he would be at this time of night, Presley stood in the middle of the kitchen but then heard muffled voices. It was faint but she padded toward the back window that overlooked the deck and the kids' swing set.

Seth. Standing outside the backdoor in his hated robe. Talking on the phone. A call he obviously didn't want her to hear. He'd just made love to her so passionately but now he was talking to God knows who about God knows what. And being secretive about it.

Whirling on her bare feet, she stomped back to the bedroom and shut the door, wishing she could slam it but that would wake Ben and Lulu. Heart thundering against her ribs and shaking all over, she stared into the mirror on the back of the closet door. The woman that looked back was pale, eyes wide and lips trembling. It was the face of fear.

Her husband was sending her a message whether he realized

it or not. He wasn't the same and he didn't appear to be happy. Maybe she had put him on the back burner after Lulu's birth and then the coffee shop. It was so easy to take a spouse for granted, although she'd never felt that Seth did that to her. Was she that selfish that she assumed he'd be there for her no matter how she treated him? He loved her. She was sure of that. But that didn't mean that he wasn't restless. He thought he wanted every day to be the same but he came alive when there was excitement and spontaneity.

Presley needed to give him that gift again. She needed to give herself that gift too.

It was time to shake things up in the Reilly household. But how?

"Everything looks clear here," Seth reported to Tanner. "Knox is patrolling around the house and my deputy Hank is watching the entries into town. If Harbaugh is close, we'll know."

Seth pulled the edges of his robe closer to keep out the chilly air. He couldn't get re-dressed before coming outside. That would have raised Presley's suspicions sky high and she was already looking at him strangely. Even before becoming a mother she'd had a highly-tuned bullshit detector, but since giving birth it was formidable indeed. Ben and Lulu weren't going to get away with anything in their teenage years.

"That's good," Tanner replied. "I talked to Dare today and he's still digging into Danny Harbaugh's past, but hopefully he'll find something or someone that might give a clue as to where he's lying low. I'd rather find him before he finds you."

"I just want him to stay away from Presley and the kids."

There was a small silence on the other end of the line before Tanner spoke again.

"You haven't told Presley?"

Seth shook his head even though there was no one to see it. "Absolutely not. Ever since Lulu's birth she's been battling terrible migraines. Last time she visited the doctor she told Presley to avoid stress. Then the doctor kind of laughed at her own advice because how can a mother of two young children avoid stress? But the doc said she should do her best which Presley tries to do with that meditation stuff, but with the coffee shop I can't put one more stressor on her plate."

It was Seth's job to protect his wife. Watching Presley go through those debilitating migraines was almost more than he could bear. He'd do anything to keep her from having a single one.

"You know she's going to find out eventually."

"I know," Seth sighed. "And she's going to be madder than a wet hen when she does but I've made the call on this. If she needs to know I'll tell her but until then I'm going with the ignorance is bliss theory."

He didn't even mention the pregnancy test to Tanner. That was a secret until both he and Presley decided to share the news. But it was one more big reason not to stress her. If anything happened to the baby because his wife was frightened or upset, he'd never forgive himself.

"She's going have your balls in a jar on the mantle, my friend."

Better his balls damaged than Presley herself.

"I'll take my chances. Also, I have some good news. My parents want to take Ben and Lulu to Graceland day after tomorrow for a couple of weeks. I admit to planting the idea but they loved it. I just have to convince Presley it's a good idea."

"That is excellent news," Tanner approved. "I know one of us will want to trail behind them but I also have a deputy who retired not long ago and he's going crazy with boredom. I'm sure he'd jump at the chance if you wanted to send him with your folks and kids. We could use the help. I can vouch for him. He's a good guy."

Seth didn't even have to think about the decision. "Call him and let's get it set up. I think the kids will be safe with my parents but you're right. I don't want to take any foolish chances."

"Will do. Check in first thing in the morning. I have the day off so I'll be taking over for Knox."

"I'm taking some time off this weekend," Seth replied. "To take some of the strain off of you guys. If Presley and I are in the same place, then only one of you need to be on duty."

"Good plan," Tanner approved. "You've been working overtime for weeks anyway and I'm sure there are projects stacking up at the house."

The first one on the list was to paint the peeling steps on the back deck. Presley had said something a while ago but he hadn't noticed until tonight.

"A million of them."

Seth couldn't get Harbaugh behind bars quick enough. This was becoming a pain in the ass.

"Listen...thanks."

"Don't mention it. I know you'd do the same."

"I would but I hope to hell I never have to."

Tanner laughed. "Amen, brother. Now get some sleep. I'll see you in the morning."

Tucking his phone back into his robe pocket, Seth tried to be as stealthy as possible entering the house. Locking the door behind him, he held his breath as he tiptoed down the hall, stopping to check on his children first, both fast asleep and looking angelic. He wanted to kiss their foreheads but if he woke them up there would be nothing but trouble. Better to err on the side of caution.

When he cautiously entered the master bedroom, the room was dark and Presley was tucked under the covers sound asleep. Tossing the robe away, he slid between the sheets next to the most beautiful woman he'd ever known. And quite the vixen, too. She'd shocked the hell out of him tonight with that black lingerie but that was his Presley. Unpredictable. Spontaneous. Never a dull moment since he'd met her. His life had been gray and staid but now it was bright and multi-colored. He had everything he'd ever wanted under this roof, and he'd do whatever it took to keep them safe.

# CHAPTER SIX

The next morning, Presley filled Seth's thermos with freshly brewed coffee and wrapped up a piece of warm toast in a paper towel so he could eat it on the road. It was early – before six – and the sun wasn't even up yet. Neither were Ben and Lulu, which was a gift from heaven. They were good sleepers but they would be awake soon and demanding breakfast.

"I've given the matter a lot of thought and I think you're right. The kids will have fun with their grandparents and it will be a good experience for them. We can keep in touch with Skype every night."

Seth's brows shot up as he accepted his toast. He'd get donuts at the station. He thought she didn't know about the donuts, but of course she did. Until last night, she'd thought she'd known everything about Seth.

"You've changed your mind? Honey, that's fantastic. Ben and Lulu are going to have so much fun with Mom and Dad."

"You made some good points and of course, I trust your parents."

Smiling, he leaned down to drop a kiss on her lips just as he did every day. "You know what I'm going to do? I've got a ton of leave saved up and I'm going to take a long weekend. Yep, four whole days. The guys owe me for covering their sick time. Maybe we can even go over to Springwood and visit Tanner and Madison. Have dinner with them or something."

Or something. Presley had some plans for her husband. She just didn't know exactly what they were yet but they had to be exciting and spontaneous. Romantic, too. She wanted to bring back the early days of their relationship. Minus the threat of death hanging over her. That hadn't been all that much fun.

"We can make plans when I get home," Seth promised, slinging his thermos under his arm and lingering in the doorway. "Do you want me to call Mom or should I?"

"I'll do it," she offered, rising up on her tiptoes to press another kiss on his lips. "I'll miss you today."

"I'll miss you, too," he said, his voice dropping low and an arm wrapping around her waist, pulling her against his hard-muscled body. "Love you, baby."

"I love you too."

She watched as he climbed into his SUV and drove down the road, his red taillights fading in the distance. Checking the clock, she had about ten minutes of quiet to think of how to surprise her husband and bring the excitement back to their marriage. It was probably going to take more than that. And more caffeine.

Seth pulled the SUV to the side of the deserted road, tucking his police radio into his jacket pocket before climbing out of the vehicle. It had been a quiet day at the station, but a call had come in about thirty minutes ago that there was a car on fire on Old Mason's Road near the big oak tree.

That's where he was standing now and he didn't see a thing. There were no other cars and this road saw little traffic.

Which meant one of three things. The call was a prank. The call was correct, but somehow the car had magically repaired itself and driven away. Or perhaps Danny Harbaugh was fucking with him. Seth didn't want to be paranoid but he had to be cautious.

Tanner's truck pulled in behind his own and the older sheriff didn't look happy at all.

"Jesus, do you have a death wish?" Tanner growled as he exited his own vehicle and stomped toward Seth. "Stay in your goddamn truck until I'm here with you, especially when the entire reason for coming out here doesn't exist. Looks like the call was bogus."

"Presley's the one I'm worried about," Seth scoffed. "I can take care of myself."

An eardrum splitting blast resonated through the stillness, like the backfiring of a truck, but this sound was familiar to Seth. Too familiar. Adrenaline pumping, he dove in between their vehicles and pulled his service revolver from under his jacket. They were under fire.

Tanner was right behind him, their backs pressed to the front bumper of the SUV as their gazes darted up and down, left and right but they saw nothing. No other shots were fired but Seth was loath to move from his position in case the shooter was simply waiting for a better opportunity.

"I think you might want to be worried about yourself as well," Tanner said between gritted teeth as he squinted up into the sun to look at the hill to their right. It was the most likely spot for cover as the rest of the area surrounding them was flat and desolate. "Looks like not everybody likes you."

Seth didn't reply, too busy concentrating on the sounds around him. Anything that would indicate the location and intention of the shooter. A twig broken under the sole of a shoe.

A huff of breath just a little too loud. Maybe the rustle of a jacket as he switched positions. All Seth needed was one tiny clue.

He didn't get it. There was nothing but heavy silence all around them except for the chirping of a few birds. On this windless day, there wasn't even the sound of branches swishing together. Reaching into his pocket, Seth radioed Hank to come up the back of the hill so he would be behind the shooter. He also told him to send Tom out to back up Reed, who was watching Presley at the coffee shop. No one was going to get near her.

Once his deputy was on his way, Seth lowered himself to the ground and inched his way toward the open field, already tired of this game.

Grabbing the sleeve of Seth's jacket, Tanner jerked him back into the gap between the trucks. "What in the hell are you doing? You can't go out there."

"I can't sit here, either."

Tanner shoved Seth against the bumper. "I don't give a fuck what you can or cannot do. My job is to keep you and Presley safe and alive, which precludes you from strolling into an open area with no cover while some asshole is shooting at you. So you'll sit your ass down until Hank comes and tells us what's going on up there."

Chuckling, Seth pushed back against Tanner. Not to move away but to let the man know that he could if he wanted to. "Maybe he's not shooting at me. Maybe he wants you. It didn't start until your ugly ass showed up."

Tanner smiled and eased his arm away from Seth's throat. "Then you're definitely staying put. I don't want anyone shot in error because of me. Seriously, what are you thinking? You know better than that."

"I just want this guy caught," Seth sighed, slumping on the cold ground. "I don't want this hanging over our heads. You guys shouldn't have to come to our rescue. Again."

Tanner just laughed and slapped Seth on the shoulder. "Are you kidding? We live for shit like this. Our jobs for the most part are boring as hell."

"So glad I could help."

"Just sit tight and wait. Running toward a shooter isn't the brightest move you've ever made."

An hour later, the only thing Hank, Tanner, and Seth had found was a spot where the tall grass had been pushed down – probably by the weight of a human – behind a large rock on the hill. That area wasn't easily navigated to, remote in nature and overgrown with weeds, but they all agreed that a truck could get back there if the driver was determined to. The ground was far too dry and hard to show much in tire tracks but there were many broken branches, as if they'd been snapped off by a high-profile vehicle.

The shooter had fired once and then hightailed it out of there. Clearly this was a warning shot. From that distance, any half decent marksman should have been able to hit his target.

Seth.

Tanner pointed to the large rock formation. "So he called in a vehicle fire, then laid in wait for you to arrive. He then shot off a round and ran before we could come after him."

"He's fucking with you, boss," Hank said. "Harbaugh has a sick sense of humor."

As long as the fucker stayed away from Presley and the kids Seth didn't care what Harbaugh did. Before they'd checked out the area, before he'd talked to Hank, before anything he'd made sure Presley was okay. According to Reed, she and Eliza were unpacking supplies today. Seth wasn't sure how Reed knew that since he was supposed to be staying out of sight but he didn't question his friend's methods.

"And he's going to continue that anti-social behavior until we can put him back behind bars," Seth replied. "So let's get that done. Have we heard from Dare? He was going to talk to Danny's parole officer."

"I've got a call in to him," Tanner said. "But he hasn't called back. Let's get to the station and figure out what we want to do next. I have a couple of ideas."

Seth had one or two of his own.

# CHAPTER SEVEN

The scent of the roses filled Presley's nostrils as she breathed in their heady and sweet aroma. Seth hadn't sent her flowers since Lulu's birth but he'd pulled out all the stops making up for the lag in time. One dozen scarlet red roses in a lovely cut glass vase. She hoped he got a deal on them because they had to have cost a fortune.

*That. Right there. I've become too practical.*

Setting them on the dining room table in full view of the living room and kitchen, she stood back and admired them yet again. She loved Seth with all of her heart, but then he did wonderfully loving things like this and that love threatened to almost overtake her. Surely no one in the world was loved as much as Seth Reilly was?

"Mama got woses. They piddy."

Presley lifted Lulu onto her hip so her daughter could get a closer look and even lean in for a sniff. "They are pretty, aren't they? Daddy sent them to Mommy."

*Because he loves me and I rocked his world last night.*

The sender of roses chose that moment to push open the front door, dropping his jacket on the floor along with his beaten-up leather messenger bag and empty thermos. Presley didn't hesitate, launching herself into his arms and pulling him down into a hot kiss that promised much more after the kids were in bed. She wanted to make sure he knew how much she loved the flowers.

"Hey, that was quite the welcome," he said huskily before kneeling down to give Ben and Lulu a hug. "What did I do to deserve it? Because I'll do it every single day."

"If you do it every day we might go broke," she giggled, motioning toward the dining room table. "But I love that you did it today. Thank you, Seth, they're beautiful."

His eyes widened and she could see that even he was surprised at how gorgeous they were. He must have ordered them over the phone instead of in person.

"Um…wow…those are really something."

She'd been so worried about her marriage but then he'd gone and done something this wonderful. Now she felt a little silly. "Thank you so much, honey. I love you."

He walked over to the flowers and studied them, reaching out to touch a velvety petal.

"Was there a card?"

Shaking her head, she linked her arm with his and pressed her head to his chest. "There wasn't. Did the florist lose it? What did it say? I bet I know what it said."

"What do you think it said?"

Keeping her voice low, her gaze flashed to her two children quietly playing with their toys. The peace wouldn't last long but she'd enjoy it while she could. "That last night was amazing."

"It was," he agreed, his fingertips brushing her cheek. "I–I'm glad you like the flowers, babe."

"I need to check on dinner. We'll eat in about ten minutes." Pausing in the doorway to the kitchen she blew a kiss to her husband. "I love you."

"I love you too."

All marriages hit bumps in the road but they were going to be fine.

✧ ✧ ✧ ✧

Hiding in the upstairs bathroom while Presley read a bedtime story to Ben and Lulu, Seth called Tanner.

"I'm going to take you up on your offer," he said before Tanner could even greet him. "Tomorrow, right after my parents get on the road with the kids, I'm taking Presley on a vacation. The sooner the better."

"You didn't think it was such a great idea a few hours ago," Tanner replied. "What's changed?"

Still furious and terrified, Seth paced the small room like a caged tiger. All his energy had built up and he had no way to burn it off. "A dozen fucking blood red roses showed up at the house today. Presley thinks I sent them."

Silence stretched out while Seth seethed, every second pissing him off more. He'd rip Harbaugh into pieces if he so much as looked at Presley.

"What did the card say?"

"No card," Seth answered curtly, sweat pooling on the back of his neck. "She thinks I was being romantic. But we both know this was a warning like the gunshot today. He's fucking playing with us. He's been watching us, watching Presley. I need to get her out of here right away. I'd take her out of here tonight but it would raise her suspicions."

"You could just tell her what's going on."

Tanner didn't know all the facts. "I don't want her stressed or upset. I'll have to tell her eventually but right now we don't know a goddamn thing about where Harbaugh is or what he has planned. I'd like to wait until we have more of a handle on all of this."

"Have you bought the tickets yet?"

"Not yet but I'm going to. I'll text you the flight number as soon as I know it. Will it be you or Reed tailing us to the airport?"

"Not sure. It could even be Dare or Griffin. I think you're doing the right thing. Get out of there and blend in with the crowd. With any luck Danny Harbaugh won't have any idea where you've gone."

Seth and Tanner ended their call and he shoved his phone in his pocket. He headed down to the kitchen where his laptop sat on the counter and pulled up a travel site. He could smell the strong floral aroma and it made him slightly sick to his stomach. He wanted to toss them into the trash but there was no way Presley would allow that and he wasn't ready to explain his actions.

Within minutes he had everything he needed – plane tickets, hotel, and ground transportation. They'd leave for the Billings airport right after he sent his parents on their way to Memphis.

"What are you doing, you handsome stud?"

No black lace tonight but she'd gone one better and was wearing one of his dress shirts, half unbuttoned, the hem brushing her thighs and showing off her fantastic legs. There was something about a woman in a guy's shirt, and he was just Neanderthal enough to enjoy the possessive vibe of her wearing *his* shirt.

"It's a surprise."

The words came out choked but then he wasn't known for being eloquent when his wife paraded around in front of him with amorous intentions.

Her brows flew up and her smile widened. "Another surprise? Seth Reilly, you are becoming almost spontaneous. What is it?"

If she only knew what motivation it had taken for him to be this spontaneous. When this was all over he'd leave it to her. She was far better at it and it only stressed him out to try.

"A trip," he replied. "A sort of second honeymoon while the kids are with my parents."

Clasping her hands together in delight, her eyes glowed. "A trip? Where are we going?"

This was the tough part. Presley was a curious person but he needed to keep the destination under wraps until they were at the airport gate. The less people knew the better. He didn't want to put anyone in extra danger because they had information on Seth and Presley's whereabouts.

"It's a surprise, baby," he chided. "You'll know when we get to the airport tomorrow."

"Airport," she breathed. "It's far enough away that we can't drive. Hmmm…that leaves a bunch of options on the table. But wait, how will I know what to pack?"

He hadn't even thought about that. "It will be nice weather, even hot. We might go to a fancy restaurant. Does that help? If you don't have what you need you can shop when we get there."

"Okay, it has stores and restaurants. That means we're not going camping."

Not after the last time he'd taken her and she'd almost been eaten by a bear. Even animals couldn't stay away from Presley.

"Not camping," he said firmly. "Someplace I think you'll like."

"I'm sure I'll love it." Her smile fell and she groaned, burying her face in her hands. "But I can't leave. Not right now. It wouldn't be fair to Eliza. We have so much work to do on the shop."

Shit, he'd forgotten all about that, not that he would admit that to Presley. She already thought he didn't take her ambitions seriously enough.

"I've got that covered," he assured her, thinking fast. "I bet Eliza and Alex would love a few days off too. When we get back I can help in the evenings so you can catch up. Ben and Lulu will be with my mom and dad. It will all work. Trust me."

She was considering it, biting her lip in thought. He held his breath as she decided, knowing that failure was simply not an option here. They were going if he had to kidnap her and tie her to the airplane seat but it would be better if she went willingly.

"Let me call Eliza," she finally said. "You're probably right that Eliza and Alex would like to spend some time together. But if she even hesitates to say no—"

"Trust me," Seth said soothingly. "She's going to love the idea. Everybody gets what they want. It's perfect."

For the second time in their relationship, Seth and Presley were going into hiding. Hopefully they'd be better at it this time, because Danny Harbaugh wasn't going to give up.

# CHAPTER EIGHT

Presley wasn't the best flyer but Seth was acting even worse. His face was pale and his gaze was darting all over the waiting area of the airport as if expecting a maintenance crew to come strolling in pronouncing the plane unworthy for takeoff. Or maybe he was watching to see if the wing fell off while it sat on the tarmac. Either way, she was surprised to see her husband so nervous. They'd flown before and he'd been fine, although he'd complained about the legroom. He was a tall man and the space between the rows didn't allow him to stretch out much, if at all.

"Flying is much safer than driving."

Brows pinched together, Seth turned his attention to Presley. "What?"

"Flying is much safer than driving." She placed her hand on his and laced their fingers together. "You seem nervous. Everything is going to be fine. It's only a two-hour flight. We'll be there before you know it."

An older woman sat across from them reading a book on her e-reader. "Maybe you should have a drink, young man. It might relax you."

"It's one in the afternoon," Seth protested but the older woman simply laughed.

"You're going to Vegas where there are no clocks. Live a little."

Presley gave a grateful smile to the woman. "She's right, Seth. When we get on the plane have a beer. My name's Presley, by the way, and this is my husband Seth. He's usually not afraid to fly."

"I'm not afraid to fly," he protested, his gaze going over her head again. "I just have a lot on my mind, that's all."

An interesting statement. What was going on in Seth's head these days? She had no idea but last night she'd thought everything was back on track. But now that she'd had time to think about it this entire trip was so out of character. One minute he'd acted like he didn't want to be married anymore and the next he was sweeping her off to Vegas for a second honeymoon. Very suspicious behavior for a man that was so regimented his closet was organized by color.

"My name's Tilda and it's nice to meet you." Tilda closed her e-reader and placed it on her lap. "Is this your first time going to Vegas?"

"Actually we got married in Vegas about six years ago," Presley laughed, linking her arm with Seth's. "We're doing a second honeymoon while the kids are on a trip with their grandparents."

"Honey," Seth said in a chiding tone. "I doubt Tilda wants to hear all about this. She's reading her book."

"Oh, but I do," Tilda replied, wearing a big smile. "It's so nice to see a young couple so happy and in love. You're going to love Vegas. So much fun. I go twice a year, no matter what."

"Twice a year? That's amazing. All by yourself?" Presley asked.

Chuckling, the older woman shook her head. "Not at all. I have a group of friends that I meet. We're all widows now and grandmas but we're not dead, if you know what I mean."

Tilda winked and giggled. What a fun and charming woman. Presley wished that she had a grandma like Tilda. What little family she had was currently doing life in a federal prison for selling arms to terrorists and trying to kill her. More than once.

"You might have to give us some tips on things to do."

Tilda eyed Seth up and down. "If I had a husband that looked like him I'd never leave the hotel room."

Presley burst into laughter but Seth didn't appear amused, shifting uncomfortably under the grandma's unabashedly admiring gaze and tugging at the collar of his shirt.

"You young people are so easy to embarrass," Tilda laughed. "When you get to be my age not much bothers you. Because believe me when I tell you that great sex is about the best thing in life." She held up the e-reader. "Of course, these days I can only read about it. But the hotter the book the better, if you ask me."

Poor Seth was blushing but Presley was having a great time. "I'm definitely going to need your book recommendations."

Tilda's eyes lit up. "I have so many. You'll love them."

A movement out of the corner of Presley's eye captured her attention. Twisting in her seat, she pointed to a crowd of people near the coffee vendor. "Seth, is that Griffin Sawyer over there?"

"No."

Frowning at her recalcitrant husband, Presley pushed at his shoulder. "You didn't even look. I think I saw Griffin."

"You didn't see Griffin."

"How do you know? You won't even look."

Sighing, Seth looked up from his plane ticket. "Fine, where did you see him?"

Presley pointed behind Seth. "Over there near the coffee."

Glancing over his shoulder, Seth shook his head. "I don't see him."

"You didn't even hardly look."

What was with her husband lately?

Seth's brows rose. "Do you still see him?"

"Well…no."

"Then how would I see him if you can't?"

He made it sound so logical but deep down she knew he was being a shit.

"Because you're taller," she explained, semi-patiently. "If you would stand up and take a look, you might see him."

With a sigh heavier than the last one Seth levered to his feet. "Fine. Now tell me where again?"

"There." She pointed to the line wrapped around the coffee kiosk. "He was standing there but looking in a different direction."

This time Seth really looked, examining the entire area. "Sorry, honey. I don't see him. It was probably someone that just looked a lot like him. They say everyone has a twin."

She could have sworn she saw him but perhaps not. "It sure looked like him. Maybe he and Jazz are visiting Los Angeles."

Seth settled back into the hard, uncomfortable chair. "He didn't mention anything when I saw him a few days ago."

"You didn't mention you saw him," Presley pointed out. This was becoming a habit. So much went on in Seth's life and she never heard about it.

Shrugging, he opened his phone and began scrolling. "He stopped by. It wasn't a big thing."

Tilda leaned forward in her seat. "If you want to go look for your friend, I'd be happy to watch your bags."

"No," Seth said loudly. "I mean, that's okay. He's not here."

Presley wanted to smack the back of her husband's head. "Seth," she whispered. "Be nice. She was just trying to help."

Of course her law enforcement husband wasn't going to allow a stranger to guard their belongings. He was suspicious of everyone. Right now, Presley was only suspicious of him. He'd been acting strange as hell. A few days ago she'd been sure he was tired of her, but now she simply thought he needed more excitement in his life. He was tired of the same-old every day. He just didn't know how to verbalize his boredom.

"I know but he's not here. Why would he be here?"

Presley didn't want to argue with her husband about all the reasons – good and bad – that could have Griffin catching a flight out of Billings. She wanted their second honeymoon to be peaceful, fun, and full of raucous sex. Lots and lots of it.

The announcement for their flight came over the loudspeaker. It was time to board. One step closer to that hotel room and Vegas, baby.

Seth didn't think the nice little old lady he and Presley had chatted with in the waiting area of the airport worked for Harbaugh but he couldn't be absolutely sure. It was for that reason he'd tried to keep Presley from becoming too friendly with her and revealing too much about Ben and Lulu but as always, with his wife it was a losing battle. People were just attracted to her funny and warm personality. She could talk to anyone about pretty much anything and he ought to know. When he'd met her they'd been talking about sex within thirty minutes of shaking hands.

And he didn't talk about sex with anybody. But he had that night. She could draw out even the most shy people and he found it a lovely trait. Just not today when he was trying to keep her from being killed.

To his relief, Tilda had been seated in another row so he and Presley ended up talking to a young woman who was going to be a bridesmaid in the wedding of a close friend who was sitting a few rows in front of them. Seth spent the flight scrutinizing their fellow passengers looking for anyone that appeared shifty or out of place while Presley quizzed the young woman about all the wedding details. Once again, by the end of the flight they'd exchanged email addresses and looked to be fast friends.

For maximum privacy, Seth had splurged on a private taxi instead of a shuttle to whisk them off to the Bellagio, and he kept an arm around her when they exited the vehicle, pulling her close as they bustled through the lobby. His gaze swept over the expansive space, taking in his surroundings. He didn't know exactly what he was looking for but he'd know it when he saw it. It might be someone staring at them for a second too long or maybe the same person coincidentally being in the same places all the time. He had to be on alert every minute.

There was no line at the check-in desk so he and Presley walked right up. He had printed out his online reservation and handed her the paperwork.

"That's Reilly, correct?" she asked, her gaze trained on the computer screen. "Seth Reilly?"

"Yes," he confirmed, looking over his shoulder. The sooner they were in the room, the better he'd feel.

"I'll need a picture ID and a credit card." The young hotel clerk behind the counter tapped on her keyboard and then frowned, her teeth sinking into her bottom lip. "Um, could you wait here, please? I'll be right back."

"Is there a problem with our reservation? Are we not in the system?"

He hated making reservations online. Didn't trust the process. That's why he'd printed out the receipt and confirmation number.

"It's fine. You're in the computer. I just have a question for my manager about your room."

The girl fled behind a glass wall as he dug his driver's license and credit card out of his wallet.

Presley leaned close to him, her brows raised in question and her voice low. "This doesn't sound good. Maybe the people that were supposed to check out of our room haven't left yet."

Seth hadn't requested anything outrageous. A regular non-smoking room with a king-sized bed that didn't overlook a parking lot.

An older man in a dark suit rounded the glass wall with the clerk on his heels. Holding out his hand, he smiled at Seth and Presley. "Mr. and Mrs. Reilly, how very nice to meet you. I hope you've enjoyed your stay in Las Vegas so far. I'm Nicholas Hammond, the manager of the hotel."

Seth shook his hand. "Nice to meet you too, Mr. Hammond. We've only been in Las Vegas for about an hour so everything is going well so far. Is there a problem with our room?"

That question had Hammond swallowing hard and looking nervous. "Yes and no, Mr. Reilly. The original room you booked online does have an issue. The guest that was staying in that room contracted a nasty stomach virus and only checked out a few minutes ago. Needless to say, the room needs...disinfecting...along with the carpets and drapes cleaned."

The manager looked a little green and Seth was pretty sure the poor guy had seen the room up close and personal.

"So…."

Hammond tried to give them a reassuring smile. "However, we are assigning you to another room. And congratulations, due to several conventions in town you're getting an upgrade from your original room category but at the same price. The only problem is that the room won't be ready for a few hours. Maybe more." Seth opened his mouth to assure the manager that the delay was fine but the man was already speaking again. "Of course, we here at the hotel want to apologize for this confusion. While you wait, we'd like you to enjoy lunch on us at one of our excellent restaurants."

It was past lunchtime but not yet dinner and he and Presley had barely eaten all day. It sounded like a great deal.

"That will be fine," Seth replied. "Are you okay with that, Presley?"

"Sounds good to me, but what about our luggage?"

"I'll have a bellman take care of your bags," Hammond said, waving to a young man with a large cart. "I can send you a text when the room is ready."

The one thing Seth had learned that when traveling you had to roll with the punches, even if someone was trying to kill you. So far there wasn't any sign that they were being followed or watched. If they'd successfully snuck out of Harper, there was no reason not to relax and have a good time. This was Vegas, after all.

Have fun. But be vigilant.

# CHAPTER NINE

"Wow, this restaurant is really nice," Presley said, looking around their opulent surroundings. From their table, they had a magnificent view of the fountains outside. "I'm crazy starving too."

The manager had given them a voucher for their meal that Seth had thought was far too generous, but now that he'd seen the prices on the menu it made perfect sense. The tantalizing aromas wafting from the kitchen made his stomach growl softly, demanding to be fed.

"It is nice," Seth agreed. "What do you think you're going to have?"

After a quick discussion comparing the pros and cons of certain dishes, they ordered their meal and relaxed with a couple of drinks. Iced tea for Presley and a beer for him. Just one. He needed to stay sharp and aware.

As casually as possible he let his gaze wander the room, studying the other diners. Once again, he wasn't looking for anything in particular, but he'd know it when he saw it. That one person who stood out, but not for the usual reasons. Something out of place that didn't make sense. He couldn't quite let his guard down but he wanted Presley to have a good time. There was no reason they both needed to be stressed.

"I feel awful for that poor person in our room," she shuddered and made a face. "But I guess it was our good fortune because now we're eating in a swanky restaurant and we've been upgraded, too. How lucky can you get?"

Kind of an ironic declaration but then she didn't know they were hiding from a madman that wanted to kill them both. Or maybe just her. Harbaugh hadn't been all that clear on exactly who he wanted to murder but Seth was going to assume it was both of them. That wasn't lucky in the least.

"We sure are lucky, sweetheart. And we have almost four days here. Have you thought about what you want to do and see? Looking back on it, we didn't do much when we were here before."

They'd been too busy getting married and then going straight to the honeymoon part of the trip.

Almost jumping out his chair, he felt her bare toes trail up his bare leg under his jeans. Thank goodness, the tablecloth covered that naughty gesture from onlookers.

"I was thinking Tilda had the right idea. Maybe I'll keep you in bed the whole time."

Then the little vixen gave him a wink that had him hard and ready. Just like that. He was past forty but he acted like a horny teenager whenever they were together. He could only hope their whole lives were like this.

And it made protecting her a hell of lot easier if they never left the room.

✦ ✦ ✦ ✦

Once in the elevator and on the way to their room, Seth was able to take a small breath of relief. They'd arrived alive and well and so far he hadn't seen anything or anyone that made him suspicious. The whole operation had almost been blown wide open when Presley had spotted Griffin, but he must have ducked behind some other passengers because Seth hadn't been able to see him in the crowd. He was grateful for the escort to the airport but now he was on his own.

When Seth did finally tell her what was going on she was going to kill him. Probably slowly and painfully, but he wasn't going to apologize for wanting to protect his wife and unborn child. His family was far too precious to him. She'd just have to be mad. At least she'd be breathing while she hated him.

"This is fantastic," Presley squealed as Seth pushed open the door to their room. Holy moly, she wasn't kidding. When the manager said they were upgraded he hadn't been kidding. "Oh my God, there's a jetted tub in the bathroom."

Seth had only seen hotel rooms like this on television.

The suite had an expansive living room with a large television on one wall, a wet bar opposite, and sunken lounging area in between. There was a dark oak dining table near the floor to ceiling windows with a panoramic view of the Las Vegas skyline that had to be even more impressive at night.

The bedroom had a large king-sized bed, a second flat screen television, two oversized chairs, and an equally amazing view. The bathroom was all shiny marble and gold, and almost as big as the sheriff's station with a tub that had Presley grinning from ear to ear. Seeing how happy she was made him feel a little guilty that he hadn't swept her off for a second honeymoon long before this. They needed a getaway and as soon as Harbaugh was behind bars he was going to take her on one. A real one. No killers allowed.

"I see you really like that tub," Seth said, wrestling their luggage onto the rack in the closet. "Someday when we redo the bathroom at home we'll have to install one."

Presley stuck her head out of the bathroom. "How old will we be when that happens? Will I be like Tilda and too old to get in and out of the tub?"

She was busting his balls.

"Are you suggesting that I procrastinate about household projects?"

Presley snorted, turning the water on full blast. "I'm not *suggesting* anything. I'm saying it straight out. Your honey-do list gets lots of items added to it but I never see anything checked off."

That wasn't true. He'd finished a project...when was that again? Okay, maybe it had been awhile.

"I'm going to get to all of that as soon as I can."

"I know, babe." Presley kicked off her shoes and they landed in a spot by the television. "I feel so...*dirty*. Want to wash my back?"

She didn't wait for his answer, pulling her shirt over her head and tossing it away before her fingers began working on the button of her jeans.

Damn, she was sexy. And goddamn beautiful. His mouth went dry as she stripped off her bra, revealing her two perfect breasts. A little fuller than before the children, but with the same pink nipples he loved to feel in his mouth. He'd always thought that after a few years of marriage the lust would die out, replaced by a more sedate affection. He was tired sometimes and they didn't do it as much as they used to, but he still desired Presley as much as he had at the beginning. Hell, more because when they did make love it was special.

Somehow she'd figured out the jets easily and the water swirled around her form as she lowered herself into the steaming water. Crooking a finger at him, she beckoned him closer like

Eve tempting Adam with an apple.

"Are you going to join me?"

The safest place for Presley was right in the room. Fuck yes, he was going to join her. Then he'd keep her here for the next four days. Pretty much exactly like their honeymoon. Tilda had been thinking just right.

Seth almost tripped on his pants as he struggled to step out of them, requiring Presley to hide her giggle at his clumsy haste. He was anxious and honestly, so was she. She'd eyed these fancy bathtubs in magazines for a long time, fantasizing about how she and Seth would play in them if they had one but never thinking they'd find it in Las Vegas. Sin City. She should have known. Sin sounded pretty good right now. Her sexy as hell husband had brought her on a romantic getaway for just the two of them and she was going to enjoy every single minute of it.

And every single inch of Seth.

His body was like a work of art, all firm muscles with dips and planes that her hands itched to explore. Wide shoulders, flat abs, powerful thighs, and a tight, cute butt that made her want to give an animalistic growl and bite one of those ass cheeks, all sculpted from helping his family on the ranch and doing manual labor out in the yard. She was sure Seth had never had a gym membership in his life, although he might have lifted weights in his youth when he'd played football.

A few drops of water splashed out of the tub when he stepped in but she had a feeling it was simply the first of a cascade that was going to baptize the floor before this little assignation was over. She made a mental note to tip the maid well.

Seth started to kneel down but she reached up and stopped

him, pointing to the large rim of the bathtub. The way the tub was situated on a platform there was plenty of room for him to sit down and be comfortable. He folded a towel and rested on it as she pushed his legs apart, insinuating herself between them and closer to her goal. Leaning forward, she ran her tongue around his flat male nipple, drawing a ragged groan from his lips before performing the same act on its twin. Just listening to the sounds of his pleasure sent a tingle of anticipation up her spine.

Scraping her fingernails lightly down his ribcage, she felt him shudder under her ministrations as she placed open-mouthed kisses on his ridged abdomen. Her tongue found the silky treasure trail under his belly button and she followed it as his cock pressed insistently against her. For a moment she thought about teasing him a little but he was already far too worked up. It could have been his arousal or the heat from the bathtub but his face was slightly reddish and shiny with moisture.

Bending farther down and careful not to slip in the swirling water, she took a long lick of his cock from base to tip, then swirled her tongue around the head a few times. Seth cursed under his breath and then leaned back, bracing himself with his hands as she took him into her mouth, keeping her lips tight and sliding down as far as she could take him until he bumped the back of her throat. His reaction made her feel powerful and sexy, knowing that she could give him this.

She had his complete and undivided attention.

Working her lips up and down his shaft as deeply as she could take him, she let her fingertips caress the sensitive flesh of his inner thigh near his groin. That was a special "spot" that always sent him over the edge. It only took a few minutes to have him gasping and groaning, completely at her mercy.

His hand cupped her cheek and he pulled her off of his cock with a pop. "Easy, honey. I want to fuck you hard and deep first."

Such a romantic rascal but they'd learned she had a kink for dirty talk, and although Seth wasn't the most loquacious man in the bedroom, he often indulged her less than pure quirk. He had a gift for it too, despite being such a fine, upstanding pillar of the community. He could be one filthy boy.

Looking up at him from under her lashes, she gave him one last lick with her tongue, feeling him shudder in return. "How do you want me, handsome?"

Full of trust, Presley placed the control of their lovemaking fully into Seth's capable hands. With all the things she needed to do and remember each day, it was sometimes so wonderful to just sit back and let him drive. Let him take the lead and make the decisions while she relaxed and luxuriated in the pleasure.

"I think I'll take you from behind, pretty girl."

Shifting from where he was sitting, he arranged her so she was kneeling in the bathtub, her elbows resting on the padding of the towel and a water jet hitting her clit. She was going to go off like a rocket with or without him.

But it would be so much better when he was inside of her.

His cock nudged at her entrance, pressing in and then re-treating, just teasing her a little. Presley tried to push back against him to impale herself but received a hard, wet smack on her ass for her trouble. Heat swept through her veins and she wriggled her bottom, hoping for another. She couldn't see it but there had to be a nice red handprint on one of the cheeks.

"Don't be in such a hurry, babe. Let's make this last."

That statement was a joke because she knew without a shadow of a doubt that he was just as close to blowing as she was. That evil jet was sending a steady stream of fizzy water right to her swollen and sensitive clit and a bar of arousal had already taken up residence in her abdomen, growing steadily with every touch from her husband. Breathing and coherent thought were becoming increasingly difficult and if he didn't fuck her soon she was going to do something drastic.

"You are such an asshole," she hissed as he pulled out again but he simply laughed and then thrust in to the hilt, making her cry out and arch her back at the sheer beauty of being so wonderfully full. No one had ever filled her the way Seth did. Their joining was perfection.

That thrust also made her shift and that devilish jet hit her at just the right angle and her channel clamped down on his cock as a mini-orgasm swept through her body, making her toes curl and her lids flutter shut.

"Jesus, woman," Seth swore. "That almost killed me."

The heat from the steamy water rose into the air, the warmth wrapping around her and keeping the chill away from her exposed flesh. Resting her head on the towel, her body still humming from her first climax, she surrendered completely to the pleasure, giving herself over to Seth's skillful touch.

His fingers reached under her to pluck at her rock hard nipples while his cock slid in and out, the sound of their skin slapping together echoing off the tile walls. His grunts mingled with her moans of approval as every stroke rubbed all the sweet spots inside of her. The jet worked its magic on her clit as he fucked her hard and fast and she was on the precipice, dangling on the side and ready to go over any minute. Her knees shook under the churning water and she would have collapsed if Seth hadn't had an arm wrapped around her waist.

She just needed...something...but she didn't know what it was. Luckily Seth knew her trembling body as well or better than she did. Lifting her torso so her back was flat against his chest, his hands covered her breasts, pinching the nipples hard while his teeth nipped at the spot where her neck met her shoulder.

"Come all over my cock, baby. You know you want to. Scream my name when you do so the neighbors know who's balls deep inside of you."

It was the dirty talk that did it, although he'd also shifted her to a different angle for the jets and that had probably helped too. Her orgasm exploded inside of her like a band playing "The Star Spangled Banner" while multi-colored fireworks blazed in the sky overhead. She did indeed call Seth's name more than once and she heard his own grunt as he too reached his peak, his hands tightening on her skin. She might have a few love bruises to show off tomorrow. Seth would be marked by her nails as well.

Well worth it.

As they came down from their high, she began to giggle as he rearranged her so that they were lying in the tub, her back to his front. Playful and happy after his orgasm, Seth pressed light baby kisses to her cheeks and eyes before pulling her in for a long, slow kiss. The kind where he tried to say everything he was feeling without saying a word. She kissed him back the same way.

*I can hear you, Seth, and I love you too.*

# Chapter Ten

"I'll get the door."

Seth darted in front of Presley, practically knocking her over in his haste to be the person that opened the door to room service. It was the same behavior that his son displayed when the phone rang at home. Ben wanted to answer it even though he didn't have anything to say.

After their sexy sojourn in the jetted tub, they'd both fallen asleep on the big king-sized bed. As working parents of young children, they simply didn't get enough sleep. When they'd awoken, she'd unpacked for both of them while he tapped out text after text, presumably to his deputies that were covering for him this weekend. By the time she'd finished, she was ready to go out and play. She wanted to walk down the strip and see the sights.

Seth, however, had been dead set against the idea, telling her he wanted a quiet dinner. Just the two of them.

*He must have romance on his mind. Me too.*

Which was fine with Presley. As much as she wanted to explore, she wanted to explore her husband's fine body even more. There would be time to be a tourist tomorrow.

But first…she missed her little munchkins. The sloppy kisses and the big hugs. Even the stubborn chins and the pleas for another cookie. Seth's parents were fabulous grandparents but she needed to talk to her babies and see for herself that they were okay. That had led to a Skype call with Ben and Lulu where she was relieved to see they were happy and content. Giggling, they gave her kisses through the screen which she tearfully returned. She was having fun with Seth but not having her children where she could see them wasn't something she was used to. After the call, Seth had held her as she'd sniffled a little bit, telling her that the kids were doing great and everything was wonderful. And he was right. It was just unusual.

When they were done, she'd ordered dinner and champagne from room service and slipped on one of her prettier long nightgowns while they waited. Worn on her first honeymoon, it was blue silk with ecru lace around the neckline, and it hugged her figure while still being somewhat demure. A matching peignoir completed the set and she knotted the belt while the waiter wheeled in the delicious smelling food. Steaks, potatoes, grilled mixed vegetables, and a decadent chocolate mousse that she was planning to spread on select areas of her skin so she could watch Seth lick it off. If she couldn't see Cirque de Soleil then she'd damn well see her husband's skillful tongue.

Seth signed the check and closed the door behind the waiter, the Do Not Disturb sign in place on the door handle outside. Presley was anticipating quite a night but she was definitely going to enjoy a meal she didn't have to shop for, cook, or clean up afterward. There wasn't a chicken nugget in sight either and that made it even more special.

"I hope you're hungry," she said, lifting the silver domes off of the plates. Even more steam wafted out and her stomach growled its appreciation. "I'm starving. Why don't you open the champagne?"

Scowling, Seth lifted the bottle from the ice bucket. "You ordered champagne?"

"I thought it would be romantic." She'd seen him drink it, although the last time might have been at Dare and Rayne's wedding over a year ago. "We're celebrating."

He frowned at the bottle as if it had done something to offend him. "You're planning to have some too?"

Perhaps her husband had hit his head recently. "Of course, I love champagne. Why would I order an entire bottle if I was planning on just watching you drink it?"

"But you can't drink it."

The way Seth said it was as if there was no question about it. It was fact. She couldn't drink the champagne. Period. End of story. So sad, too bad. Reaching into the recesses of her memories, she tried to remember the last time she'd drank champagne. Perhaps she'd embarrassed herself and got sloppy drunk, singing bad karaoke and telling everyone how much she loved them.

"Why?"

"Because you can't," Seth said again, this time more firmly. "It wouldn't be healthy."

"But just for me? Not you?"

Placing the bottle back in the ice bucket, Seth moved closer and reached for her hands.

"You don't have to pretend, Presley. I know. I was hoping you'd tell me this weekend."

Now she was completely confused. She wasn't pretending about anything. Carefully placing the silver lid back on the dinner plate she gave Seth all of her attention.

"Tell you what?" she asked, watching his expression closely. Whatever it was that he thought she was keeping from him, he didn't seem angry or upset about it. On the contrary, he was looking at her tenderly, and even his touch was loving and gentle.

A step closer and this time he leaned down to brush his lips softly over hers.

"About the baby."

*The baby. The baby. The baby?*

"The baby," she repeated carefully, trying on those words for size. "So you know all about the baby?"

He nodded and tugged her into his arms, holding her tightly against his body. "I found the test in the trashcan, or rather outside of the trashcan when Fergus dragged everything out of it the other day. I've been waiting for you to tell me."

*Oh no... Oh God no.... He thought... Shit.*

*Is this why he's been acting strangely?*

But he didn't let her speak, his own words rushing out like a tidal wave of emotion. "I admit that I was shocked at first because we'd talked about this and said no more, but then I really thought about it and I have to say that I'm happy about it. I mean, you're a great mom and any baby would be lucky to have you." He held up his hand as she opened her mouth to talk...stop him. Anything but let him go on and on. "I know it's not going to be easy, honey. What with my crazy hours and helping out more on the ranch since Dad retired. Add in you starting your own business, but I know we can do this. Ben will be in first grade by the time the baby comes and Lulu can go to Mom and Dad's a few days a week. They're always saying they want the kids more. And I'm going to be more help around the house, I promise. I know I make plans and then sometimes I don't see them through but I'm going to do better."

Tears stung the backs of her eyes and she had to blink to keep them from falling down her cheeks. The sweet, loving, wonderful, romantic fool. He'd been thinking about this for days and had said absolutely nothing. Didn't he know her? She couldn't have kept it a secret for five minutes, let alone days or weeks. It just showed how much the thought of having a third child had scrambled his brains.

Now she had to burst his beautiful bubble and she felt like the worst person in the world to do it. She should have thought about the pregnancy test in the trash but honestly it hadn't crossed her mind. She'd had too many things to think about on her to-do list to think about what Seth might discover if for some reason the dog dragged the trash through the house.

*Suck it up, buttercup. You can't let him go on thinking this.*

Taking him by the hand, she led him over to the couch, setting next to him on the cushion. She kept a hold of his hand, stroking his knuckles with her fingertips in what she hoped was a soothing motion. Because she was about to upset him. No doubt about that.

"Seth," she began, her voice trembling with a combination of disappointment and fear. "Honey, I'm not pregnant."

Her husband didn't say anything for a long moment, seemingly not comprehending her words.

"What? I saw the test."

"I'm not pregnant," Presley said again as gently as she could. This was going to shock him no matter what but she could at least be kind about it. "The test you found in the trash wasn't mine. It was Eliza's. You know that she and Alex have been trying for the last few years. She was late and came over, nervous about taking the test. She's had so many come out negative and I think she just wanted a friend's shoulder to cry on when this one did too. But this one...didn't."

The air seemed to go out of him and his whole body seemed smaller. "Oh. I...I'm happy for them."

Running her fingers over his square jaw, she didn't take her gaze away from him, watching every nuance of his expression intently. "Are you okay? I'm so sorry that you thought that test was mine. It never even occurred to me that you would. Eliza took two tests that day. One she wrapped up and took home to show Alex and the other she put in the trash. We were both so excited for her I didn't even think about Fergus dragging it out and spreading it all over the bedroom. I'm so very sorry, babe. Can you forgive me? I never meant to put you through something like this."

Never in a million years would she have done something so cruel on purpose. She'd ripped the rug out from under him and she felt horrible. She couldn't apologize enough and she'd be making this up to him for a long time.

Shaking his head, Seth sucked in a breath. "It's not your fault. Of course you couldn't have foreseen what would happen. I could have spoken up that day as well but I was just so shocked. I wanted you to have your surprise announcement like you did with Ben and Lulu."

He still didn't look okay, his skin sort of pasty.

"I'm still sorry," Presley insisted. "I had no idea you were thinking that I was pregnant. It explains so much."

It really did. All the strange behavior now didn't look so weird. He'd been freaked out about a third baby.

But that left them at a crossroad.

They'd decided two children was enough but apparently, Seth was maybe now thinking he wanted a third. Something she hadn't given any thought to since they'd make their decision and given away the bottles and the crib. He'd even promised to get a vasectomy, although he'd found about a half dozen excuses for postponing it. Perhaps it hadn't been the idea of having his boys worked on; it had been the thought of no more babies that had made him delay. Did he only agree to stop at two because that's what she wanted?

Rubbing the back of his neck, Seth grimaced. "I was shocked at first and felt kind of guilty. I know I was the one that was supposed to be taking care of protection."

Giggling, Presley reached up to briefly kiss his mouth. "That's something we never seem to have time for but it also explains why you haven't been worried about it the last few times."

A smile curved his lips and he chuckled along with her. "I thought the barn door was already open so to speak, but that doesn't explain why you didn't think about it."

A true statement. She hadn't been thinking about it at all. It literally had not crossed her mind at any point. Was that a Freudian thing? Did she secretly want another baby? Or was her husband such a stud she could barely form words and sentences, let alone actual logical thoughts?

"I can never think straight when we're making love."

She couldn't lie about it because he was well aware of how he affected her. Talented asshole, but she loved every minute of it.

Her handsome husband grinned in response. "If it makes you feel any better, I'm not thinking all that clearly when we're together either."

Her throat tightened and she couldn't stop herself from asking. "Still?"

"Still," he whispered, lifting her onto his lap and wrapping his arms around her so she could rest her head on his shoulder. "And forever. Baby, you've got to know that I go crazy for you. I can't get enough of you."

She traced patterns on his chest with her fingertip. "I was thinking that maybe...you might be bored. That I wasn't exciting enough anymore, not as unpredictable and spontaneous."

Laughing, Seth shook his head. "Trust me, babe, you're still a bundle of trouble. My life hasn't been the same since the day I met you and I don't want to go back."

"You don't miss the order and control?" she teased, remembering that first day in the office when he hadn't wanted to make any changes. He'd had a big stick up his butt and it hadn't been easy to extricate it. "You don't miss the peace and quiet? If we had a third child you might never get another good night's sleep ever again."

Seth groaned, presumably at the thought of many sleepless nights. "Am I an awful person to say that I'm kind of relieved that you're not? I do like a good night's rest."

"You're not terrible," Presley insisted. "We both know that there would be some wonderful things about having another baby—that's why making the decision was so hard. Do you–do you want to reopen the discussion?"

Shaking his head, Seth tightened his hold around her. "No, I think we made the right decision for us and our lives, but if you were pregnant I just want you to know that it would be okay."

If it happened they'd be fine. They'd adjust and welcome the new baby into their lives. There was more than enough love in the Reilly household to go around.

"So this is why you've been acting so strangely lately," Presley laughed. "I've been thinking that you were replaced by some sort of clone or maybe a well-crafted artificially intelligent robot. Lately you've been doing some weird stuff. Like the other night, for example. Why were you out on the back porch in your bathrobe talking on the phone?"

In a split second Seth went from happy and smiling to an expression carved from granite, any mirth or contentment wiped away. Her husband was like this so rarely it immediately set

Presley on edge, goosebumps rising on the flesh of her arms.

She'd been right. There was something going on. Something besides a baby. And it wasn't a positive thing either.

"You might as well just tell me because I'll find out sooner or later."

Levering up from the mattress, he rubbed at his forehead and paced the space in front of the sofa. She let him gather his thoughts, not pushing him to speak before he was ready. Seth liked to get his ducks in a row. Finally, he paused and turned toward her, his hands in fists at his side.

"I've been acting this way because Danny Harbaugh was paroled from prison about a week ago. I killed his wife and he's sworn vengeance."

It was the worst part of being a sheriff's wife. Never knowing if he'd come home at night. A chill ran up her spine but she was determined not to show him her unease. She was strong and she could handle this. She had every day since she'd married him.

"He's threatened to kill you?"

Scraping his fingers through his hair, Seth closed his eyes for a long moment. "Kind of, but it's more than that." His eyes opened and he pinned her with his gaze. "Baby, he's threatening to kill you. He wants you dead and that's why I brought you here. To get you out of Harper."

# CHAPTER ELEVEN

Presley was absolutely livid and if her handsome husband had any sense at all he'd be afraid. Very afraid.

To keep information like this from her was damn near unforgivable. Suddenly her transgression with the pregnancy test didn't seem like such a big deal. She'd only been guilty of not thinking something through; he was guilty of lying. Something they'd sworn they would never do in this marriage. So far as Presley knew they'd keep that promise.

Until now.

He'd patiently explained the situation right down to the flowers not being from him and she'd tried to listen without judging or interrupting. When he was finished he sat down on the edge of the couch next to her, his hands on his knees as he waited for her to speak.

"So Danny Harbaugh wants me dead?"

"Yes."

"And our children?"

"I don't think Danny Harbaugh even knows we have children but just in case I decided to be safe and send them with Mom and Dad. They have Reed and a bodyguard following them. Basically Harbaugh said he wants to take away the people I love."

Now Presley had a whole new reason to worry about being separated from her children. This entire situation was getting better and better with each passionate moment.

"And all your friends are trying to find this guy in Montana?"

"Yes." Sucking in a breath, Seth snuck a glance at Presley. "Are you mad?"

"Very," she said between gritted teeth. "You deliberately kept this from me. Like I wasn't someone who has been through this before but like I'm *the little woman*."

Their relationship had been predicated on being partners and Seth had thrown that concept out of the window.

"I told you why I did that," he protested, hopping to his feet again. "The migraines, your blood pressure, and then the pregnancy. If anything happened to you or the baby because of the stress I never would have forgiven myself. Look at it from where I was standing."

She could hear the plea in his voice but at the moment she wasn't quite moved by it. A lie was a lie was a lie. His argument was that it was a lie by omission and he'd done it because…

"So you did it for my own good?"

"Yes," he replied but then he thought better of it. "I mean, no. I did it to keep you safe and healthy."

"Because I couldn't handle the truth? I was too weak?"

Seth's face was red with frustration. "You're twisting my words."

She shook her head. "I'm just repeating what you've told me. I don't want to tell you what to do, Seth, but if I were in your shoes I'd admit that you, the manly man in your infinite wisdom, decided I wasn't strong enough for all of this. Arguing all the reasons you were right to do it isn't a winning strategy here."

"I was worried about you physically. I was worried about the baby," Seth said, the words coming out more like a groan than an actual sentence. "I know that you could handle it mentally."

"Thank you so much," Presley replied sarcastically. "Thank goodness you thought I wouldn't faint with fear and go hide under the covers. I feel so special since you believe in me so much."

"I was worried about your migraines." Seth's voice had risen dangerously.

She pressed her fingertips to her temple. "I didn't have one before but now I do."

Seth threw his hands up. "What do you want me to say? Mea culpa? I should have told you? I'm not sure I would have done anything differently, Presley. I thought you were in the early weeks of pregnancy and I wanted to protect you. End of story."

"My being knocked up isn't a Get Out of Jail Free Card."

His feet were planted and his arms crossed over his chest. He was dug in for the duration.

"I did what I did to keep you safe. I'd do anything for you, Ben, and Lulu up to and including giving up my own life. You can be mad but I know I did the right thing."

"Then why were you so scared to tell me?" She wagged a finger at him. "Because you knew you had fucked up, but now you want brownie points for being all protective alpha male. I'm still pissed off and I don't feel a bit guilty about the pregnancy test in the trash anymore because that was just an oversight. This was a bald-faced lie."

They were getting nowhere. Seth wasn't going to back down. He hated to be wrong or admit a mistake. They could discuss this later when she'd had time to cool down. She could understand his reasoning – a little – but she had to make her point known. He better not do it again. She wouldn't be treated as *lesser* because she was a woman. She wasn't fragile or weak.

Because there was a fact much more important than Seth being a jerk. Someone wanted them dead. There was a man out there hunting them like prey and here she was in a hotel room in Las Vegas while her babies were in a vehicle headed for Memphis. Her motherly instinct was screaming that she needed to be with Ben and Lulu, protect them with her own body if need be.

"I didn't lie," Seth said with a heavy sigh. "I just didn't tell you everything."

She was done with this topic. There were bigger fish to fry.

"We might as well eat dinner before it's ice cold, then we need to talk so we can figure out what we're going to do. From now on, I need to be a part of these discussions. I'll leave the cop work to all of you but it's my ass on line just as much as yours."

Seth nodded, seemingly relieved she wasn't still angry. She was, but that was a luxury she didn't have at the moment.

"I'm going to send the boys a text. I'm anxious to hear if Dare has found out anything about Harbaugh."

"I have my own agenda," she informed her husband as she sat down at the table, unfolding the linen napkin on her lap. "Ben and Lulu. I need to know what you've set up to keep them safe. Then we need to double it and talk about going to get them. I need to hold my children, Seth. I need to protect them. I'm their mother."

Seth was breaking Presley's heart but he wouldn't be budged on this. Ben and Lulu were safer away from them than with them. It wasn't that he didn't want to be with his babies; he most assuredly did, but right now anyway, they were better off with their grandparents.

"We can't go get them," he said again, wishing he had better news for his lovely wife. "We have bullseyes on our backs and we'd only be putting them in the line of fire. They're with my parents, Reed, and Tanner's deputy. They're safe. Far safer than they'd be with us."

Presley was sitting at the table, dinner long ago cleared away. Her lips trembled and her eyes were bright with unshed tears. His own heart was being shredded into a million pieces but he had to stay strong.

"I want to be with my babies," she whispered, her voice tortured and making him feel even worse than he already did. It was as if he'd physically ripped Ben and Lulu out of her arms.

"So do I," Seth assured her, kneeling in front of her, his palms resting on her thighs. He had his friends on speaker phone to help him convince her that she wasn't thinking all of this through. "Believe me, I want them with me too but honey, it's too risky."

Presley's gaze flickered to the phone where Griffin, Tanner, and Dare waited on the line.

"What do you think? Do you agree?"

None of them three men answered immediately but eventually Dare cleared his throat to reply.

"I do agree," the other sheriff replied. "If Rayne and our child were in this same situation I would, reluctantly I admit, separate them. I know your instincts are telling you something far different, Presley, but Seth is right. It's safer for them if they're not with you."

Rayne had just given birth to their first child, a sweet little girl named Cherish that had her daddy wrapped around her tiny fingers. For Dare to say that he'd separate mother and child was a compelling argument.

Hopefully.

Tears spilled onto Presley's cheeks and Seth's chest tightened painfully. Lifting her up, he sat back down in the chair and situated her on his lap. "I know, baby. Cry it all out. I know this is bad and I wish I could make it better. I'm so sorry about all of this."

But he couldn't and that was tearing him apart inside. He wished he could make everything better for his wife and children but it was times like these that reminded him that he couldn't. And he hated that. He felt…powerless.

It didn't help at all that this was his fault. It was the job and he'd long ago become used to it, but then most of the time it didn't affect his family. Not this way. At most they had to put up with his lousy schedule but a death threat was something far worse.

"I want them to be safe," Presley gasped between quiet sobs. "But I'm their mommy, I should be keeping them safe. Me."

"I know and I feel the same way," he said as soothingly as possible. "Mom and Dad are taking good care of them, I promise. They're being watched all the time."

Sniffling, she scrubbed at her red and swollen eyes. "All the time? Every minute?"

"Every second," Seth vowed. "Tanner's guy and Reed are working in tandem. They're not going to let anything happen to Ben and Lulu."

Presley relaxed slightly in Seth's arms and for the first time since finding out about Harbaugh she looked almost peaceful.

"I trust Reed." She leaned forward to speak into the phone. "I'm sure your deputy is good too, Tanner, I just don't know him personally."

"I can vouch for him," Tanner said sympathetically. "But I know that probably doesn't make you feel any better right now,

Presley. Just know that we're all going to do whatever it takes to keep you, Seth, and your children safe and alive."

Clearing his throat again, Dare spoke up. "Which brings us to the next topic. Danny Harbaugh. I did some unauthorized digging into the case file when he attempted to rob that bank. You're going to want to hear this. It changes everything."

Seth's ears perked up. "I'm listening."

Presley swiped at her tears. "I'm listening, too. What is it?"

"I haven't had a chance to tell anyone this but Seth, you didn't kill Lyndsey Harbaugh. The ballistics from the bullet taken from her chest didn't match your gun."

That wasn't possible.

"I shot her. I saw it happen."

"The timing made it seem that way but there were several guns going off at the same time, yes? You, Harbaugh, plus your deputies? That's a lot of firepower bouncing around a small alleyway."

Seth could still see the scene in his mind. "Are you saying that one of my deputies did it? Because I'm not going to throw them under the bus."

"No, I'm not saying that. What I'm saying is that the bullet didn't match your gun or any of your deputies. It matched Harbaugh's. Danny shot his own wife. It was probably a ricochet."

# CHAPTER TWELVE

"It doesn't really change anything." Presley gave her husband an apologetic look. "I'm sorry, Dare, but it's true."

She was shocked that her voice still worked after the crying she'd done. The entire time she'd been on the run with Seth when they first met she'd been scared, but that had been literally nothing compared to the fear that had struck her heart when she realized that this Danny Harbaugh might go after Ben and Lulu. Frankly, she didn't like the idea of waiting around like a sitting duck either, preferring to find this asshole and get him out of their lives.

But no one had asked her opinion yet.

"It doesn't change anything," she said again when none of the men replied. "This guy doesn't know the truth and I don't think it would make any difference if he did. He'd still blame someone else for what happened. He'd just say that he wouldn't have been shooting at all if Seth wasn't firing at him. Nothing is different."

To his credit, Dare didn't argue. "You make a good point. Harbaugh isn't going to react like a normal person would. We already know he doesn't take blame well. He blames the cops for him going to jail instead of himself."

"Have you found out anything from his parole officer?" Seth asked, still keeping his arm around his wife, hoping it provided some modicum of comfort. She was a strong woman but the children were her weakness. His as well, but he needed to be the strong one.

"He checked in with his parole officer that first day but not since," Dare replied, a grim tone in his voice that came through the phone clearly. "The authorities talked to Harbaugh's older brother Eric to see if Danny tried to contact him but the answer was no. From what I've been able to dig up, there's no love lost between them. He said that if he heard from Danny he'd let them know."

"If Danny was desperate, it might not matter that he and his brother weren't close," Griffin pointed out.

"I don't even remember a brother or any other family member at the trial," Seth said, shaking his head. "I think the only person Harbaugh had in the world was his wife."

"And he shot her. Now he feels all alone." Presley rubbed at her swollen eyes. "Do they think the brother is telling the truth?"

"They do," Dare said. "He's as opposite as he can possibly be from his brother. I checked him out and I can't find even a parking ticket. He owns a small computer consulting firm. He's not rich but he makes a decent living. He was married for awhile but he's now divorced. No kids. He and the ex still get along, from what I can tell. All my research into him showed a rather boring, workaholic guy that has tried to stay as far away from Danny as possible."

Interesting how the same upbringing had created two people so different.

"So we're back where we started," Griffin said. "We look for

Harbaugh or any of his minions while Seth and Presley keep their eyes open for anything out of the ordinary."

That made Presley snort. "We're in Vegas. Everything is out of the ordinary."

"How about you just keep your eyes open?" Tanner laughed. "Stay alert for anyone who has an inordinate amount of interest in you. Harbaugh may not be working alone."

There was one thing she needed to know now that her second honeymoon included a death threat. "Are we stuck hiding here in the room? I was brought here with the promise of fun but if you all think it's too dangerous, I guess I can just order room service and watch television."

Honestly, it kind of sounded peaceful and relaxing. There was a little part of her hoping they said yes.

"I don't think so," Seth replied, bursting that balloon. "We have no reason to believe that Danny Harbaugh even knows where we are. Until then I think we can move around as long as we're cautious. The guy isn't stupid and I don't think he would open fire in a crowded casino."

"In the meantime, be alert at all times," Griffin said, his voice reflecting the grin that was probably on his face. "Romantic, huh?"

It wasn't exactly what she'd planned but it wasn't the worst thing in the world.

Presley slid into bed next to Seth and turned on the television, flipping through the channels as her husband tapped away at his phone. Probably talking to Tanner or one of the other men working to keep them safe. She appreciated how they'd dropped their own lives to come to her aid but she still felt like she was waiting for something to happen. It went against her nature to sit around and allow life to happen to her.

Her new nature. Until she'd met Seth and almost been killed by her stepsister, waiting around for something to happen in her life had pretty much been her modus operandi. Now she knew better but here she was…waiting for some criminal asshole to hunt her down.

Landing on some news channel, she tossed the remote to the side.

"I'm serious about this trap idea. I hate waiting around."

Before when she'd mentioned it Seth had rejected the notion immediately, not even allowing her a hearing. This time, however, he appeared to be considering it, or at least realized that she wasn't going to give up without a discussion.

"I know you're anxious. I understand that. But what you're suggesting is incredibly dangerous, babe. It could get you, me, or our friends killed. Friends don't get friends dead. It's kind of an unwritten rule."

"I'm serious." She turned so she was lying on her side, facing him. "It doesn't feel natural to just sit here and wait to be murdered. This is not your natural state, Seth, so don't say that it is. You're a man of action. You determine a course and you go for it."

If she thought her little speech was going to motivate him, she was wrong. Instead he scowled and shook his head.

"We're not talking about hunting down cattle rustlers, we're talking about your life, Presley. I'm not risking that now or ever." Reaching for the remote, he turned off the television. "And no one is going to be murdered, dammit. No murders."

His huffy attitude struck Presley as amusing and she found herself laughing at the absurdity of the entire situation until tears leaked from her eyes, but this time not because she was sad or angry. It was – in a crazy macabre sense – hilarious. Or she might be hysterical.

"Please share with me what is so fucking funny," Seth ground out as she slapped a hand over her mouth to contain the giggles. "I could use a good laugh right about now."

"This. Us." She hiccuped a few times. "Think about it, Seth. What are the odds of two people being hunted even once in their lives? But you and me? It's like déjà vu all over again. A crowded tourist city to hide out in. Looking over our shoulders constantly. Your friends helping us out. It's like we attract murderous psychopaths. We deserve each other. If we'd married anyone else we just would have pulled them into our dark and dangerous lives."

Smiling too, Seth wrapped an arm around her waist and pulled her close, tucking her into the curve of his body. She pillowed her head on his shoulder and breathed in his warm and comforting scent that never failed to make her feel safe and loved.

"Then I guess it's a good idea that I fell in love with you on that road trip," Seth chuckled. "I'm not sure anybody else would be quite so brave as you've been. You also haven't blamed me once for this, even though I know it's all my fault. It's my job that puts you and the kids in peril."

"You didn't blame me last time," she pointed out. "This is your job and you love it. It would be pretty crappy of me to bitch and moan when I know you'd step in front of a bullet for me or anyone that you loved, really. You were born to be a lawman. I'd never ask you to quit."

They were quiet for a long time, listening to the hum of the air conditioner while he stroked the sensitive flesh of her arm.

"I know my job is hard on you," he finally said. "I know what you have to sacrifice."

Funny how they'd never talked about it. Some things in

marriage never needed to be said, but she was beginning to realize that there was a whole hell of a lot they hadn't said to one another over the years. Not necessarily because they didn't need to be said but because they either never had the time or the subject was touchy and emotional. Better to avoid it.

And life made it so easy to ignore. It was times like this when it was only the two of them and they had nothing but great yawning stretches of togetherness that afforded them with the opportunity to talk. Although whether that was a good or bad thing was an open question.

"I do worry about you," Presley admitted, glad that she didn't have to look her husband in the eye at the moment. He'd see the fear that lurked there every time he left the house to go to work and she wouldn't burden him with that. He was doing something he loved and that wasn't something every person could honestly say. "But I know that you're smart and good at what you do. You don't take unnecessary risks. I know that you want to come home to us every night."

"Still...being a sheriff's wife is no great prize. The hours are terrible and the money is shit, and that's not even counting the people that shoot at me."

Now he was simply exaggerating. Their house on the ranch was owned free and clear, as were both of their vehicles. Most of their extra money either went to Ben and Lulu's college funds or into savings for retirement. "Most of the time you work a regular workday just like everyone else, and as for the money it's not bad either. We aren't starving or dressed in rags."

In fact, they'd been able to use some of their savings for her half of the coffee shop. The rest of the money was from what she'd banked when she'd sold her old, burned down house in Florida. The house had been a write-off but the property was in a desirable neighborhood and had been quickly snatched up.

There had also been a few thousand dollars from the insurance settlement on her blown up car.

Seth ran his fingers through her hair. "I just want you to be happy."

"I am happy so you can forget about trying to get rid of me. I'm here for the duration."

She'd fight any woman who might get some ideas regarding him. It wasn't the most enlightened attitude, but when it came to Seth she wasn't all that civilized.

If this Danny Harbaugh thought she was going to roll over and play dead he was sorely mistaken. She was ready to fight. Fight for her husband, Ben and Lulu, and for her life.

No one was going to take her family away from her.

# CHAPTER THIRTEEN

I t was always the same.

Seth and Presley had breakfast down in one of the hotel restaurants and, as usual, someone had struck up a conversation with Presley in the buffet line. The woman who looked to be in her twenties had asked Presley a question about the muffins and then they were off to the races. The young woman was here with her girlfriends on a sort of half vacation-half bachelorette party and had regaled Seth's wife with tales from last night when they'd attended a male strip show. They'd urged Presley to go as well at her earliest opportunity.

Hell no. There was no way he was going to allow his wife to ogle a bunch of oiled-up muscle men waving their dicks in her face to loud music. At least he assumed that's what would happen. He'd only seen that movie and even then against his wishes. Presley had dragged him there on one of their date nights. He'd spent the entire film slumped in his seat with his hand over his eyes, shoving popcorn into his mouth.

"Is it always like that?" Griffin asked later in the morning when they were all on a conference call. Seth and Presley had gone back to their room and were debating how to spend their day.

"It is," Seth confirmed quietly, giving his wife a loving look. "You get used to it after awhile. So much for keeping a low profile. She just attracts people wherever she goes."

"Then her new coffee shop should be a raving success. You'll get customers from three neighboring counties," Griffin laughed.

"I'm glad you find this amusing," Presley sniffed, plopping down into a chair near the window so she could look out. It was a warm and sunny day. "I can't help it, you know. I don't control other people. As much as I'd like to."

"How do you do it?" Dare asked. "I'm being completely serious with this question. Do you think it's something you do or simply some vibe you put out into the universe?"

"I have no idea," Presley sighed. "People just gravitate toward me, although I do think it's because I'm a people person in general. If you want more people to talk to you, Dare, you could try smiling more."

Presley had said it gently and it was clear Dare Turner hadn't taken any offense, instead laughing at her suggestion. "I didn't want to know how to get people to talk to me. Far from it. I wanted to know so I could make sure I didn't do whatever it is that you're doing. People are a pain in the ass."

Presley grinned and laughed at their grouchy friend. "Does Rayne know you feel like this?"

"She does," he confirmed. "And she's given up trying to reform me. I'm a lost cause."

"Well, I don't know what I'm doing. I don't go out of my way to speak to strangers. They find me. It drives Seth crazy."

Not as much as in the beginning.

"It's not so bad. We've met some interesting people over the years," Seth admitted. "It's only when someone is trying to kill you that it's annoying."

"Speaking of someone trying to kill me. Shouldn't I know what this Danny Harbaugh looks like so I can watch for him?" Presley asked. "For all I know he was the guy at the waffle station who asked me if I knew if it was going to rain today."

"What did you say?" Tanner asked.

"That I didn't know for sure, but we're in the desert so odds were no."

Seth had been standing right there, too. Presley was gorgeous but she didn't usually realize when men were hitting on her.

Wanting to smack himself in the forehead, Seth scrolled through his phone. She was absolutely right and he should have thought of it without her having to ask. He flipped the screen so it was facing Presley. "This is Harbaugh. Does he look familiar?"

She squinted at the screen and then reached for the phone to take a closer look. Studying the photo, she finally shook her head. "Not even remotely, but if he's such a smart criminal then wouldn't he wear a disguise? Change his hair color? Grow a beard? Maybe wear glasses?"

"He's no mastermind. He got caught," Griffin replied.

"But he managed to pull off several bank robberies before doing so," Tanner pointed out. "He might think about altering his appearance but then you and Seth could do that too."

Last time they'd gone through this Presley had changed her hair color and style but Seth was hopeful that they didn't have to go to that extreme.

They continued chatting about plans for the day, Seth and Presley keeping a vigilant eye out for anything that didn't look quite right if they ever managed to leave the hotel. To Seth's relief nothing seemed amiss this morning and he didn't have that crawling feeling on the back of his neck that they were being watched. Sneaking out of town might just have worked.

Dare quietly cursed on the other end of the line. "I just got a text and I think you all need to hear this. Danny Harbaugh is dead. His body was identified in a meth lab explosion outside of Bozeman."

Presley wanted to believe what Dare was saying but it seemed too good to be true. She didn't much like the fact that she was relieved that another human being was dead, but when that same human being had been hunting her down she was going to give herself a pass. She would rather that he'd been captured and returned to jail but his decisions in life had put him on another path. He hadn't been at a meth lab to sell encyclopedias.

"They're sure it's him?" Presley pressed. "I mean, if it was an explosion, how are they sure?"

Apparently Dare had a second phone to his other ear trying to get the details while she peppered him with questions and he was being quite patient about it. If this was true it was a huge relief. Ben and Lulu were safe and so were she and Seth. Her little family was going to be fine.

"Okay," Dare came back on the line. "I have some more information. There was an explosion and it's early yet but the cops think it was an accident, not intentional. They were able to quickly identify Harbaugh because not only did he have a wallet in the back pocket of his pants, the body that they recovered had a very distinctive tattoo on his chest that wasn't completely destroyed in the explosion so I don't think there's any doubt here. Harbaugh is dead."

Everyone was quiet as they absorbed the news.

"So it's over," Tanner finally said. "Looks like you can enjoy your second honeymoon after all."

The call ended shortly after with effusive thanks from both her and Seth. These men were true friends and Presley promised to have them all over for dinner very soon along with their wives. She wanted to show her appreciation for all they had done, although cooking them a meal seemed like such a small thing in return. How do you thank someone for dropping everything and protecting you and your children?

Restless, Presley slid off of the couch and walked over to the window where she could see the bustling streets below. "What do we do now?"

A slow smile slid across Seth's face and his eyebrows waggled up and down.

"Vegas, baby."

The slot machines were being kind to Presley. She'd managed to stay even or a little ahead today. Nothing big. She wouldn't be retiring anytime soon but she might be able to afford a steak dinner out with her husband tonight.

On their second honeymoon. A real one now that she could relax and enjoy herself. She'd talked to her in-laws and the children already, not revealing that they'd been under the protection of a couple of bodyguards. They were having a great time and she'd loved the kisses Ben and Lulu had given the computer screen.

"You have the best luck. I think I'll let you do all the gambling today."

Poor Seth was having a rough time. He hadn't gambled much but when he had he'd lost. He'd made a joke about being lucky in love but she could tell when he was frustrated. If he wasn't having any fun, she wasn't either. She didn't honestly care about the slot machines, She just wanted to spend time with him.

"We can go on up to the room if you want. I wouldn't mind a nap or we could just laze around and read or watch television."

Or the two of them could try out that jetted tub again.

"Are you not having a good time?"

He was so worried about her, he'd forgotten that this was his honeymoon, too.

"I don't think you're having a good time. Seriously, let's go back to the room. Peace, quiet, and sleep sounds like a vacation to me. Maybe your luck will be better later."

His brows pinched together. "I wanted you to have fun."

"I always have fun with you." He hesitated as if he wasn't sure she was serious. "It's fine. We can order room service. You know how I love to do that."

A smile tugged at the corners of his mouth. "You do enjoy that. Okay, let's head on up."

"I might take a bath too."

Now she had Seth's full attention. His arm around her waist tightened and he leaned down to press a kiss to her temple.

*I love that bathtub. They can bury me in it. In about sixty years.*

"The peace and quiet is lovely," she said as they strolled hand in hand through the casino and toward the elevators. "This is going to sound crazy but I miss the noise and mayhem."

Like last week when Ben had fed his grilled cheese sandwich to Fergus and the poor dog didn't poop for two days. Presley had called the vet in a panic after she'd realized he'd eaten the whole thing but the doctor had assured her that Fergus would be fine. Then the kindly older man had regaled her with a tale about how his own dog had somehow managed to get the refrigerator door open and wolfed down most of their leftovers from Thanksgiving dinner.

Chuckling, Seth pressed the elevator button. "I miss them

too, honey, but I know they're having the time of their lives and being spoiled rotten by my parents."

"That's what I'm afraid of."

It was going to be difficult to get the kids to follow rules after a few weeks of being without them.

The entered the elevator and the doors began to close when another man, breathing hard, managed to slide in at the last minute. Brown-haired with glasses, the man flashed a smile their way and pressed his floor button.

"Whew, barely made it," he said, wiping at his brow. "Having any luck today?"

Clearly Seth didn't like being trapped in a small box with an unknown person. This was his lawman persona and it didn't matter that no one was trying to kill her anymore. This was all about his cop instincts. He was a cynical bastard and saw ax murderers behind every ficus plant.

Seth probably didn't even realize what he was doing as he crowded her so she was placed behind him in the corner of the elevator. He was in protector mode and she'd do well to let him do whatever he felt he needed to do, because she knew from experience there wasn't any way to talk him out of it. If he even admitted to the behavior.

"We're doing fine," Seth said curtly after a long pause. The tone in which he'd answered didn't invite further conversation and Presley hoped that the man received the message.

Sadly, he didn't. "Can't get over this dry weather. I'm from Florida. Tampa, actually. Ever been there? Humid as the devil's armpit."

Seth's reply was to push her tighter into the corner so all she could see was his wide back. The other guy could have been brandishing a weapon and she wouldn't know.

But…she had to admit that it was weird that the stranger had brought up Tampa, her former home. Was it one of those strange coincidences?

"No," Seth answered again, this time almost growling the reply. Luckily, he didn't have to say any more as the car came to a stop and the doors slid open.

"You folks have a great day," the man said cheerily, exiting the elevator. "Enjoy your stay."

The doors closed and Seth stepped forward to press the button for their floor several times as if to make the car go faster. A muscle jumped in his jaw. No elevator ride had ever been longer than the two floors to their room.

"What the fuck was that?" she asked in exasperation as he pressed the key card against the sensor of their door.

Seth stomped over to the wet bar and pulled out a bottle of water. "I don't know. Don't you think that was weird?"

Presley wrapped her arms around Seth, placing her head on his chest. This whole Danny Harbaugh situation had taken its toll on her husband. Even now when they were safe he couldn't seem to relax. Maybe he was having as hard a time believing it as she was. They'd been at a thousand percent stress and then suddenly...nothing. The threat was gone and life was normal again. They needed to give themselves time to get used to the news.

"It was probably just some friendly tourist. That's all. We've been paranoid as hell on this trip and it's made us crazy and suspicious."

Seth was shaking his head. "He mentioned Tampa..."

"The Tampa Bay area has about a half million people in it. One or two of them might have decided to come to Vegas on vacation this weekend."

Rubbing the back of his neck, Seth's expression was anything but happy. "I'm overreacting, aren't I? It's just..."

"I know," she said. "I'm having trouble adjusting too. A few hours ago, we thought we were being hunted down and now we're supposed to just go have fun and pretend it didn't happen. Maybe we should just cut ourselves some slack and have a long soak in that bathtub."

She didn't need casinos and neon lights to have a great vacation. She only needed Seth.

And a nap. And maybe that jetted tub. And room service.

# CHAPTER FOURTEEN

S eth and Presley spent the rest of the day and the evening in
the room ordering room service for dinner, watching
television, and lazing in the jetted tub. They enjoyed the peace
and quiet, finding time to talk about topics that never seemed to
be discussed in their day to day rush.

Hopes for their children, dreams for their future, and the
fears too. Bad things couldn't be avoided in life and for the first
time Seth expressed his fear about his parents growing older.
Right now they were active and in excellent health but there was
a good chance that wouldn't always be the case.

She'd fallen asleep in her husband's arms safe in the
knowledge that he was as committed to their life together as she
was. They were lucky to have found each other and she'd never
take that for granted. They'd also promised to make more time
for just the two of them. It wouldn't be easy but they needed to
make sure that they didn't neglect their relationship.

The next morning they ended up at the same breakfast buffet, both of them tired of staring at the same four walls of their
hotel room. Presley was itching to be more active and Seth had
suggested a walk to see the sights.

Presley was enjoying her waffle when she spied the strange man in the elevator sitting several tables away. "There he is."

She kept her voice low so only Seth could hear her but the restaurant was so loud she probably needn't have bothered. The place was buzzing with activity and the clatter of dishes and silverware muffled any nearby voices.

Glancing out of the corner of his eye, Seth's expression didn't change but he nodded acknowledging that he'd heard her.

"I see him now. If I turn around he'll know we're looking at him. You have a better vantage point. Is he looking at us?"

She shook her head, trying to keep her gaze somewhere to the man's right instead of directly on him. "No, he's just eating and drinking coffee by himself. That's weird, don't you think? Who comes to Vegas alone? I guess his friends or family could be sleeping. It's still early in the morning."

Now she was acting paranoid. It was just a man and he was paying absolutely no attention to them, peacefully minding his own business and munching on a piece of bacon. Of course she was going to see him if they were staying in the same hotel.

Seth drank the last of his orange juice. "Are you done eating?"

Was she? The cinnamon roll was delicious but this was her second helping and if she continued eating this way while they were in Vegas she wasn't going to fit in the airplane seat on the trip back home. On the other hand, she and Seth had been...active...between the sheets, so that had to burn a few calories.

"Let me finish this and then I'll be ready to go."

Grinning, Seth reached across the table with his fork. "I'll help you."

Slapping his hand away, she popped the remaining half into her mouth, relishing the flavor.

"You'd think after all these years together you'd know not to touch my food."

"You'd think after all these years together, you'd share every now and then," Seth complained but in a good-natured way. "Just once."

"I gave you two children. You want my food too?"

"Cranky."

Dabbing her napkin daintily at the corners of her mouth, she gave him a smirk. "Yes, you are. Are you ready to go?"

Throwing her purse strap over her shoulder, she and Seth strolled out of the restaurant and straight for the front doors without a backward glance. That man wasn't going to get another second of her attention. This was her vacation, dammit.

They meandered slowly down the sidewalk, taking in the sights of the city that they hadn't seen the last time they'd visited. Presley loved people watching and this was a fabulous location for it. As usual, a few fellow tourists struck up a conversation with them as they watched the dancing fountains outside of the hotel. The couple was from Los Angeles and was in town just for the weekend. He liked to play blackjack and she liked to sit out by the pool and read mystery novels. Even Seth chatted with them for several minutes, completely relaxed in a way she hadn't seen in quite awhile.

Eventually they continued on their explorations, pausing in front of The Venetian. She'd wanted to take a gondola ride but hadn't mentioned it to Seth, assuming he wouldn't want to do something so cheesy.

"These hotels are so cool." Presley snapped a few photos on her phone to send to Eliza and Marion. "I love that each one has its own special theme. Where to next?"

He pointed to The Venetian hotel. "Right here."

That grin. He had that shit-eating grin on his face.

"Here?"

"You want to take a gondola ride, don't you?"

Her mouth fell open in shock. "How did you know?"

"Honey, you aren't that good at hiding things. You kept looking at the brochure in the airport. I could tell from the look on your face that you wanted to do it."

But...

"You don't have to. I know you hate stuff like this."

He really did, although he rarely protested.

"But you like it and that's good enough for me. Besides, what could be more romantic for a second honeymoon than a gondola ride?"

"You are the bestest husband ever."

"I know. Please remember that the next time I do something stupid."

Giggling, she placed her hand in Seth's. "Lead on."

She'd follow him anywhere.

Later they were walking along the Strip when Presley spied a display of teddy bears in the window of a shop. She'd been searching for something to take back as a little gift for Ben and Lulu.

"Aren't they cute? We could get Ben that one and Lulu that one."

They were multi-colored and wearing tiny t-shirts that said "Las Vegas." A little touristy but they were adorable. Lulu would love it and so would Ben, although he was getting to the age where he didn't want everyone to know he still liked his stuffed animals. There were t-shirts in the shop as well, so she could get Lulu the bear and buy something else for Ben.

Seth nodded his approval. "They'll like whatever we bring

back but you know the way they argue. Whatever it is needs to be the same. Get them both a bear or a t-shirt or a hat but make sure it's identical. Remember the Great Candy Bar Incident last year? That got ugly."

She did indeed. Marion had given Ben and Lulu each a "fun size" candy bar the day before Halloween, except that Lulu's was a Milky Way and Ben's was a Three Musketeers. Nothing had been *fun* when they realized that their candy wasn't "equal".

"Good point. I'll dash into in there and grab their souvenirs while you get us a couple of coffees."

The fancy coffee place was just down the street but she'd seen that sign a block and half ago. She needed caffeine and lots of it.

"I could argue that coffee this late in the day will keep you up at night but I know I'd be wasting my breath. The usual?"

She gave him a playful wink. "What will we do if we can't sleep? We might have to find an outlet for all of our energy."

Presley was kind of counting on not wanting to go to bed early. At least to sleep.

"When you put it that way…"

"And a muffin," she called over her shoulder as she entered the souvenir shop. This should only take a few minutes but it would check off a big item on her to-do list.

Darting into the store, it only took a few moments to make her selection. T-shirts for the both of them in a neutral yellow with splashes of blue and green. She paid cash and was back outside before Seth was finished getting coffee. Tucking her package into her oversized handbag, she headed up the sidewalk toward her husband. She wouldn't mind checking out the coffee shop's display of mugs as she'd been giving her own store's space quite a bit of thought while she was here. She needed to talk to Eliza about perhaps moving their retail section closer to the entrance. Maybe they even needed to have some t-shirts printed up with their logo on the off chance a tourist wandered into town.

Presley had only walked a few feet when she felt something pointy in the small of her back and a male hand grasped her upper arm.

"Don't say a word," a voice from behind her cautioned, his breath hot on the back of her neck. Her heart jerked in her chest and her breath caught in her throat. This wasn't supposed to be happening. "Just smile and walk and everything will be okay. I don't want to hurt you. I just want to talk."

Where in the hell was Seth?

# CHAPTER FIFTEEN

It shouldn't have taken that long in the coffee shop for a vanilla latte – for Presley – and regular black coffee – for Seth – but the woman in front of him seemed truly baffled by all the choices in front of her. It was as if she'd never purchased a coffee in her life and she'd quizzed the barista on each option before finally deciding on a caramel machiatto.

Pushing the door open with his arm, he juggled the two hot drinks in his hands as a couple tried to squeeze past him without waiting for him to exit the shop. Presley had to be finished with her shopping by now and it only took a second for him to spot her walking slowly up the sidewalk.

But it was all wrong.

Her gait was stiff and her lips pressed so tightly together they'd disappeared into her face. Another closer look had him cursing under his breath. That man. The one they'd met in the elevator and then seen this morning at breakfast...

*That man* was standing right behind her whispering into her ear with his hand wrapped around Seth's wife's arm.

This asshole was going to lose his fingers. Maybe the entire arm. He'd be pulling back a stump when Seth was through with him. White-hot fury burned in his chest and coursed through his veins. There was fear as well but he didn't even acknowledge it. Later he'd give in to it once Presley was safe and unharmed. She didn't need a frightened, cowering husband. She needed a damn hero and he wasn't going to let her down.

He needed to listen to his soldier and cop instincts, eschewing all the doubts and fears that were crowding his head right now. He didn't know quite what was going on but his wife was scared and that's all that mattered. Clearly, she didn't think she could walk away from him freely with the man's grip on her upper arm.

Who in the fuck did he think he was, touching Presley?

Better question...why?

Danny Harbaugh was dead. So who in the hell was this sorry son of a bitch?

*Doesn't matter. Get Presley. Make her safe. Find out his story after.*

A flicker of relief passed over her pale features as Presley's gaze met his. The man was so intent on her he hadn't noticed that Seth was standing about twenty feet away. Seth wanted to keep it that way. The element of surprise would be on his side.

The man and Presley passed Seth and, tossing the drinks into a nearby garbage can, he followed behind them. Close enough to watch them but far enough that he wasn't right on the guy's heels. They appeared to be heading back to the hotel, which was good news as far as Seth was concerned. He had an idea and all this asshole had to do was cooperate.

His anger simmered for four more blocks as he followed them, hating every single fucking second of it but knowing he needed to wait for just the right moment. Not only did Seth need to get Presley safe he also needed to find out why this man was following them. Or for whom.

*Plus, I can't put a beatdown on this guy in public.*

When the man and Presley turned into the lobby of the hotel Seth closed the gap, getting right behind them. The back of the man's neck was sweaty and there was literally no humidity, which meant he was nervous.

Good. He ought to be. Scared, too.

Seth had at least forty pounds and five inches on this guy so it wasn't going to be a fair fight, but then he didn't really give a shit. The man never should have touched Seth's wife. Big mistake. One he was going to regret.

Things were going exactly according to plan as Presley and the man approached the elevators. The only other people waiting were two young men who couldn't tear their gazes away from their phones and weren't paying a bit of attention. The doors slid open and that was when Seth made his move, ramming his body right into the man's side and knocking him away from Presley and into the elevator car with Seth right behind him. Presley had staggered in surprise but managed to find her balance and move aside as the doors slid shut.

Now it was just the three of them.

Shoving the stranger up against the wall, Seth felt a glow of satisfaction as his fist landed in the man's soft gut. A groan escaped from his thin lips and he immediately doubled over, gasping for breath.

This was going to be easier than Seth had thought. The guy had no fight in him. He didn't come back at Seth, only holding up his hands over his face and cowering.

"Hey! Wait! I'm not armed and I didn't do anything. Don't hit me!"

The stranger straightened but the anger in Seth hadn't yet been assuaged. He gave the man a right hook to the jaw that sent him sprawling on the elevator floor, blooding trickling from his mouth. With the man out of commission, Seth was able to turn his attention back to his wife.

"Are you okay?"

Seth inspected Presley head to toe, paying close attention to where she'd been handled on her arm. There didn't appear to be any bruising but if there was...

"I'm fine. I thought he had a gun in my back. He said he didn't want to hurt me and that he just wanted to talk."

The elevator doors slid open and Seth jerked the man up by his collar, much to the shock of the older couple standing in the hallway waiting to board. Their eyes wide, they took a step back as if unsure of the entire situation. Seth gave them both a sheepish smile as he rousted their stalker out of the car.

"So sorry, folks. Our friend here had a little too much to drink and made a pass at the wife of a jealous man. I doubt he'll do that again. We're just taking him back to the room to get him cleaned up."

Chuckling, the couple nodded and entered the elevator as Seth dragged the half-unconscious man down the hall to their suite. Whoever this was, he was about to tell Seth his deepest secrets.

Who was he and why was he following them?

Presley fetched a towel from the bathroom and pressed it against the man's bleeding lip as Seth used the one and only tie he'd packed to restrain his wrists to a dining chair. Their stalker blinked and groaned finally noticing that Seth was hovering above him, glowering down menacingly.

"What was that for? I didn't do nothin'."

"You touched my wife," Seth growled, pacing the area right in front of their prisoner. "You shouldn't have done that."

Any other day, Presley would have enjoyed her husband's

alpha male display but they weren't getting to where they needed to be. The man wasn't going anywhere for awhile and the most important thing was to get information from him. Seth could beat the shit out of him later if he still wanted to.

"Seth, I think he's ready to answer a few questions," Presley suggested and her beloved growled again. Red-faced, his shoulders were rising and falling rapidly. He needed to calm the hell down. "Okay, I guess I'll go first."

"Who are you and why did you shove a weapon in my back and try to kidnap me?"

"My name is Stan. Stanley Wallace and I'm a private investigator."

That brought Presley up short. The last thing she'd been expecting was that he was a PI.

Seth leaned in aggressively so he was face to face with Stan. "What do you want with my wife?"

Sweat beaded on the private investigator's forehead as his gaze darted between Seth and Presley.

"I just wanted to talk to her," Stan replied loudly. "To both of you, really, but I figured it would be easier to get her to talk. You're a big guy."

The PI was obviously intimidated, which made this entire scenario bizarre as hell. What could he possibly have to talk about to both of them?

"Who is in the mood to rearrange your face for touching and scaring my wife," Seth retorted. "Now you better start talking."

"I didn't mean to scare her. I swear. Listen, I'm a nice man who believes in non-violent solutions. Shit, I donate to Greenpeace. I don't even have a weapon. I was using my iPhone and pretending it was a gun."

And she'd been fooled. Now she was mad, too.

"What do you want?" Presley asked again. "If I were you I'd

answer before my husband loses his patience."

Stan shook his head fearfully, more sweat pouring down his pale face.

"All I want to know is where Danny Harbaugh's money is. That's it. Once you tell me I'll be out of here and you'll never see me again."

What in the...? Danny's money? Since when did Harbaugh have money and why would they know where it was?

Looking over at her husband, Seth appeared to be as puzzled as she was.

"Danny's money?" Seth turned and walked over to the windows and stared out, seeming to catch his breath and calm down slightly. "I have no idea what you're talking about. What money?"

"The money from the bank robbery," Stan said, his tone urgent. "It was never recovered by the cops and that's you. By the looks of this hotel suite, you must have it."

Presley didn't owe this man an explanation but it was actually rather amusing that he thought they had bank robbery cash because they were living large in Las Vegas.

"This was an upgrade by the management because of a problem with our room," Presley explained. "We don't have Danny's money. But even if we did, why would we give it to you? What claim do you have on it? It should go back to the bank."

"It's not for me," Stan said, bending his head so he could wipe his damp cheek on the collar of his button down shirt. "It's for the man who hired me. Now that Danny's dead, the money belongs to him."

Scraping his fingers through his hair, Seth turned back from the window.

"Okay, that's a good place to start this conversation at the beginning again. Who hired you to find us and the money?"

Stan smiled weakly as if the answer was going to make everything better.

"Eric Harbaugh, Danny's brother."

# CHAPTER SIXTEEN

S ome days were easier than others and this day was turning out to be a real bitch and a half. Seth had tried to listen as patiently as possible to this Stan Wallace, private eye for hire. The story was almost too wild to be believed. And yet...the guy was frightened for his life and at this point didn't have much reason to lie. Knowing the man was no physical threat, Seth had untied him, although he kept him in the chair far away from where Presley was sitting on the couch watching the interrogation. He wasn't stupid enough to think she didn't want to join in or interrupt but to Seth's surprise she sat back and let him do his job.

After emptying his pockets, the PI had shown him his driver's license to prove he was telling the truth about his name. Then he'd shown him the text messages back and forth between him and Eric Harbaugh that appeared to back up his claims. Seth had quickly sent a text to Dare to check Wallace out as quickly as possible.

"He's scared to death," Stan declared. "The cartel wants their money and they don't care how they get it. Danny dealt drugs for them while in prison and some of the merchandise disappeared and they didn't get paid. They're not happy about that. Since Danny is dead, they say that his brother is responsible for his debts and that he has to pay up."

That part did make sense. Cartels believed that debt lived on after a person died and that their relatives took on the obligation. But there were still unanswered questions. A bunch of them.

Seth retrieved a bottle of water from the wet bar and handed it to Stan. The poor man had to have sweated out at least a quart.

"Now let's start from the beginning again," Seth instructed. "Eric Harbaugh called you a few days ago?"

Stan nodded as he gulped down half of the bottle in one go. "He did. Said he got my name from a friend who used me in their divorce. I specialize in finding cheaters and bringing in the evidence. I told him that this was out of my expertise but he was adamant that he wanted me to do it so I took the job. He offered me three grand. That's a lot of pictures of philandering husbands and lying wives."

"And you did what after he hired you?"

"I checked the newspaper accounts of the robbery and capture," Stan said with some pride in his voice. "That's where I found out about you. You arrested Danny Harbaugh but the money was never found. It didn't take a rocket scientist to figure out that you probably took it, especially as Danny didn't get the cash first thing when he left prison. I assumed he didn't have the money no more because someone else did."

That was one theory but there were others. Certainly Seth had been questioned by federal authorities but he'd been easily cleared. He'd never been out of sight of not one but two of his deputies, plus the reporters that had been chasing the story behind them in their news trucks. The whole situation had been a clusterfuck that could have managed to get several innocent people killed.

"Me?"

"Yep." Stan nodded excitedly. "It all made sense. A small town cop sees more cheddar than he's ever seen in his life at one time. It was a no brainer."

It was like being trapped in a Philip Marlow novel. Cheddar? This guy really loved being a private eye.

But now Seth was pissed off again but for an entirely different reason. This man's casual assumption that everyone was dirty and criminal didn't sit right at all. Maybe it was his profession that made him cynical as hell but Seth was going to straighten him out quickly.

"No brainer, huh? If it was so fucking obvious, why didn't Danny kill me and get the money on day one?"

From the slack look on Stan's face, he hadn't really thought all of this through to its obvious conclusion.

"I–I don't know. Maybe he didn't know you had it. Maybe he just knew it was gone."

"But if it was obvious to you, shouldn't Danny have figured it out?" Presley asked, from her perch on the couch. It was the first thing she'd said in quite awhile but there was a smugness in her tone that hadn't been there before. "If Seth is the clear choice, why didn't Danny come get the money? Especially with a cartel threatening him?"

"I–I don't know."

Criminals were dumb but sometimes regular citizens were, too.

"So let me get this straight," Seth said, trying to keep his voice calm when he really wanted to smack some sense into this guy. "Danny gets out of prison and instead of killing me, Presley, and my two kids and getting the money he goes and hangs out with his loser meth cooking friends where he's blown up by accident. In the meantime, I'm in a nearby town spending Danny's ill-gotten gains on a trip to Vegas, not bothering to hide from the authorities or this cartel that I've stolen evidence from a crime scene. That was your hypothesis?"

Stan was sweating again despite the cranked air conditioning. "When you say it that way—"

"It doesn't make a lick of sense," Seth finished for him. "Just so we're all clear here, I have no fucking clue where the bank robbery money is. None. It wasn't with Danny when I arrested him. We searched for days and never found it. And Danny sure wasn't saying anything. As far as I know he was the only one who knew where it was."

Presley stood and walked over to where Seth was sitting across from Stan, placing her hand on his shoulder. "What do you think happened?"

Shrugging, he sighed. "We looked for quite awhile but never found anything. My theory was that he called someone while I was chasing him and gave the money to them for safekeeping. Probably one of his less than honest pals, although I doubt they set that cash aside for him for when he got released. My guess is that money is long gone, spent by his so-called friends."

Stan wasn't giving up without a fight. "He swore revenge on you. I saw it in the papers."

"Because he thinks I killed his wife, which I didn't. Not because I had his money. If he wanted money to pay the cartel he wouldn't have bothered with the subtle threats he was sending me and Presley when he got out of prison. He was drawing it out and playing a game, enjoying the cat and mouse. If it was only money he wanted, he just would have come and shot me. I don't think he gave a shit that he owed money to the cartel."

Harbaugh was the kind of guy who thought he could always

figure a way out of a situation. Too much self-confidence and not enough brains to go with it.

"This is bad. So bad." Stan slumped forward with his head in his hands. "The cartel hasn't given Eric much time to get the money."

Seth guessed that they sounded scary but they'd waited this long. They'd probably wait a few more days. But from what Dare had been able to find Eric Harbaugh was a pretty straight-laced guy, almost boring, and a couple of enforcers from a drug cartel would have scared the shit out of him. Not surprising he'd hired some help.

But Stan? Jesus, Eric should have chosen better. This guy wouldn't last five minutes with anyone from that cartel. He'd be spilling his bank and Facebook passwords along with his mother's maiden name and the name of his favorite pet.

"Seth," Presley said softly. "Can I talk to you over there for a minute?"

"Wait here," Seth commanded Stan who just nodded, looking weathered and beaten. The man had had a crappy day, that's for sure. "Do not move one inch."

Following his wife over to the bar area, he kept one eye on their private investigator, still not trusting him. He believed Stan was telling the truth but that didn't mean he wouldn't try and run away.

"If Stan believes we have the money, couldn't the cartel think so too? If Eric doesn't give them the money, could they come after you? Or us and the kids?"

*Shit. Shit. Shit.*

"It's possible," Seth replied carefully. "Not probable though. They're going to put this on Eric Harbaugh and squeeze him hard. They won't care where he gets the money as long as he gets it."

"And if he doesn't," she pressed. "What will they do then?"

Rubbing the back of his neck, Seth groaned. "Honestly? They'll probably kill him, after a period of torture, of course, just in case he's holding out on them."

Hell, they'd probably kill him whether he paid them off or not.

"Then what? Do they write off the debt or do they come after the bank money? And how many other people think we have the money?"

"I don't know," Seth confessed. "But no one has bothered us all these years so I don't think there's an army of people sniffing around for the cash. I think we're safe, honey."

"I don't like this. Not at all."

He didn't like it much either but he had to be realistic. Most people were going to think that Danny Harbaugh had hidden that bank money.

Presley crossed her arms over her chest, her little chin lifted in determination. Fuck and double fuck. Seth knew from long experience that he wasn't going to like what she had to say.

"You know what I think we need to do?"

"No," he said heavily. "But I don't think I can stop you from saying it."

"We need to talk to this Eric Harbaugh and tell him we don't have his money so he leaves us alone."

That wasn't the horrifying suggestion that he'd assumed it was going to be. From the dossier that Dare had put together and Seth had reviewed, Eric Harbaugh lived in Billings so it wouldn't be a big deal to stop there when they flew back home tomorrow.

"And then we need to help him find that money."

Now that...that was what Seth was afraid she was going to say.

# CHAPTER SEVENTEEN

After a few hours of scaring the crap out of Stan, Seth had finally let the grateful man go with a promise that they wouldn't tell the cops on him if he didn't tell on Seth for hitting him a few times. Dare called back and was able to affirm before Stan left that what he'd told them – at least about himself – was true. He didn't have a criminal history and frankly he didn't look frightening or intimidating in the least.

"What do you think Stan will tell Eric?" Presley asked Seth later that night as they finished their room service dinner and lounged on the bed. It had been an eventful day. "Do you think he'll tell him about us?"

Seth finished punching in another text to Tanner. He'd been on and off the cell phone almost constantly since Stan's hasty departure. The private eye had said he was heading back to Montana tonight since there was no more reason for him to be here in Vegas.

"Yes and no. I do think he'll tell him he saw us but I doubt he'll tell the person paying him that he was made." Seth had given poor Stan some career advice this afternoon. Stick with divorces. Stan seemed to agree. "He won't want to admit that we know why he was here. Assuming he was telling the truth about Harbaugh but I don't think he was lying about that. He seemed sincere. I think he'll just tell him that we don't have the money."

"Do you think Eric will expect us to show up?"

That had Seth dragging his nose out of his phone and giving her all his attention.

"No, because we're not going to show up and see him."

It was obvious that her husband was losing his patience. Since Stan Wallace had told them his story, Seth hadn't wanted to listen to anything she had to say.

Tough. Unless he left the hotel room, Seth was a captive audience now.

"One," she said, counting out on her fingers as he groaned and leaned back against the stacked pillows and headboard. She'd shut up about it all over dinner but he didn't honestly believe that she'd dropped it completely? Didn't he know her at all? "One, the cartel might believe that you have the money. That's one good reason to do it."

"Presley, I do not want to talk about this. Can't we just enjoy our last night in Las Vegas? Let's go dancing."

She wanted to talk and he was stonewalling her. He hated to dance and the only reason he was offering was to distract her. Did he honestly think it was going to work? She wasn't Ben or Lulu.

"Two," she went on as if he'd never spoken. "The authorities might believe you have the money and come after you someday."

"I cannot believe you're still talking." Seth scraped a hand down his face before turning toward her. "Listen to me closely, my wife, please. The government does not think I have the money. I have been cleared."

"That's what they said," she argued. "But maybe they're just waiting for us to buy something lavish. Maybe they're watching you."

She was paranoid just thinking about it.

"And who is *they?*"

"You know...the cops."

Sighing, he closed his eyes and smacked the phone against his forehead. "I'm the cops, baby. Me. If I was under investigation, I'd know it. It's been years since that robbery and I've heard nothing. Believe me when I say that a police organization cannot keep a secret that long. No one thinks I have the money."

She couldn't argue with that logic. Yet.

"I'll give you that one but that doesn't mean that the cartel doesn't believe it."

Seth had that patient look on his face again. The one he would wear when he was explaining something he didn't think she'd understand.

She hated that expression.

"The cartel doesn't care where the money comes from, babe. They don't care if Eric Harbaugh has to mortgage his house or sell his car or maybe a kidney. They just don't give a shit. It is not their mode of operation to go after some random person because they might have money, especially when that person is a cop. Whether it's the bank money or cash from Harbaugh's mattress they don't give a shit. Money is money."

"What if Eric Harbaugh tells the cartel that we have Danny's money?"

Rubbing his chin, Seth actually looked like he was considering her question. For real this time.

"That is a possibility, I will admit. Although they could think he's just lying or trying to delay. I also don't think they'd come after us themselves. They'd make him do it. They don't want to be seen by a cop as part of all of this. They're careful like that. That's how they stay in business."

Even if Seth and Presley weren't in danger anymore...Eric Harbaugh was. And from what Dare had found, he was a decent guy trying to make a living. But he'd had the bad luck to have a sibling who was a criminal.

Just like her.

"They're going to kill him, Seth."

He shook his head and held up his phone. "They are not going to kill him. I've already sent several messages to the guys about this. We can get the poor bastard some protection to keep him alive."

That sounded fine for awhile but eventually the cartel was going to lose what little patience they had. "How long can you keep him safe? The rest of his life? That doesn't sound practical."

"We don't have to keep him safe forever. Just long enough to put the leaders of the cartel in jail."

"And just how do you plan to do that? If it were easy I would imagine it would already be done."

"Tanner has contacted Jason Anderson who used to work for the DEA. He has some buddies that work the Montana area and he's sure they know about this cartel. We'll simply give them a hand bringing the head honchos in."

He made it sound so straightforward. As if putting drug czars in jail happened every single day. Easy peasy lemon squeezy, as Ben would say.

"Once again, I ask how? What's different today than yesterday when it comes to busting this drug ring?"

It was right then that she knew the answer that Seth wasn't saying. She wasn't a stupid person and she should have figured it out before. Damn.

"No," she said, smacking the newspaper she'd been reading down on the bed. "You can't."

Growling in frustration, Seth tossed his phone onto the nightstand. "He has a choice. He doesn't have to do it."

Presley shook her head. "He doesn't have a choice. He's scared and thinks he's going to die a grisly and painful death. He won't be thinking straight."

She ought to know. In the days following her car explosion logical thought hadn't come easily.

"The agents will explain it all to him, baby. Both sides. He'll be completely informed of the risks so he can make the right decision for himself."

Sometimes Seth was a complete optimist, blind to the hard truths in the world.

"You cannot use Eric Harbaugh as bait to catch a drug cartel, Seth Reilly. He's some kind of computer geek, not a super spy. He'll get himself killed."

"The agents are going to make sure they do everything in their power to make sure that doesn't happen."

"And if it does?"

Twisting around, Seth took her face in his hands and leaned forward so they were almost nose to nose. She could feel his warm breath on her cheek and smell the tang of his body wash, both scents comforting when she was agitated. She'd once compared his scent to putting on a favorite flannel shirt, toasty and soft and so familiar. Now she simply thought he smelled like home.

"If Eric Harbaugh does nothing, there's a good chance he's going to end up dead. As in not alive or breathing. I feel sorry for him that he had such a lousy brother but he's in a bad spot. If I were his friend and advising him I'd tell him that he's safer with the Feds than on his own. He can't handle this by himself.

Just like you couldn't handle Randall and your sister by your-self."

That was underhanded, bringing up her past. When she was Katie... She barely remembered those days. They seemed so far away, as if they'd happened to another person. In a way, they had.

"And then what happens when he puts the big guys in jail? Won't he be a marked man?"

Seth's phone chimed and he picked it up to check the message. "He can go into witness protection and start a whole new life, separate from Danny Harbaugh."

"What if he doesn't want to go?"

Chuckling, Seth leaned down and dropped a kiss on her lips. "It didn't work out so badly for you."

Her life was much better now than it had been before. Still...

"I feel sorry for him. He didn't ask for any of this."

"Neither did you, honey."

That was true but it didn't help Eric Harbaugh. There had to be another way.

# CHAPTER EIGHTEEN

Keeping an eye on Presley at the coffee kiosk in the airport, Seth growled in frustration. He was on the phone with Tanner and the news wasn't good.

"You're kidding me, right? Please say that you're kidding me."

"I'm afraid I can't," Tanner replied heavily. "According to Jason who talked to the DEA agents, they've declined to intervene in this matter."

Government-speak, which always meant bullshit.

"Declined to intervene," Seth repeated, trying to keep his voice down. There were throngs of people everywhere and the last thing he needed was for someone to report him to security for being out of control. "What in the fuck does that even mean?"

"Listen, I know this sucks but Jason explained that the DEA has a man deep undercover in that cartel and they're using them to get an even bigger fish based out of New York. If they bring down this group then they ruin all the work they've put in for the larger bust. I'm really sorry but Jason said they won't budge."

Pacing the small area by the newspaper stand, Seth took a

few deep breaths. Being pissed about it wasn't going to change anything except his blood pressure. When the government dug in its heels there wasn't a thing he was going to be able to do about it.

"And they won't protect him?"

Another heavy sigh from Tanner. "They're not in the business of personal protection. They suggested to Jason that Eric Harbaugh hire a bodyguard."

"If he could afford that then he could probably just pay off the cartel."

"I'm sorry, my friend. It's bad all around. Dare dug deeper into Harbaugh's finances and the poor bastard is in debt from starting up his consulting firm and the ex-wife got the house in the divorce. Hell, he even cleaned out his 401K for this business venture. His assets consist of a late model Ford F-150 truck and a collection of Star Trek memorabilia, valuation unknown. Unless the head of the cartel is a Trekkie I doubt that's going to do much good."

No wonder Eric Harbaugh had sent an investigator after Presley and himself. He was a desperate man. He'd probably used his last three grand.

"Presley is going to have a cow when I tell her this. She identifies with this guy because of her sister and his brother. She wants to help him."

"I feel for you," Tanner replied, sympathy in his tone. "You know...shit, never mind."

Seth knew what his friend had been about to say. That Seth could indeed help Eric Harbaugh.

But that wasn't going to happen.

The money was probably already gone and spent.

"Bite your tongue," Seth scolded. "I don't want to get involved with another man's problems."

"Seems to me you're already involved," Tanner chuckled. "Presley makes a good point, though. The cartel just might think you have the bank money. It could put you and your family in danger."

"That's a low probability."

But it was all Seth had been thinking about since Stan had spilled his story.

"You're the most careful son of a gun I know, and you don't leave much to chance."

Jesus, Seth hated his life right about now.

"Let's say that I do decide to help Eric Harbaugh find the money. And then let's go out on a limb and say that I do actually find the cash. We can't give it to the cartel. I have to give it back to the authorities. You know that and I know that. It won't help him."

"True," Tanner conceded. "But it would help you. Don't try and say that this hasn't bugged you all these years. There was no closure on that case. Somehow Danny hid that money while you were chasing him and he had to be damn sneaky to do it because you were right on his tail. That has to piss you off."

His friend had hit a little too close to home for Seth's comfort.

"Are you working for my wife?" Seth said a little too loudly. A few passersby slowed down and frowned at his aggressive tone. "I mean, it sounds like you're on her side."

"I'm not on anyone's side. I'm just playing devil's advocate to try and get you to see all the sides to this situation. I don't think it's as black and white as you'd like to believe it is. Look for the money. Don't look for the money. It's up to you. But don't pretend that you don't give a shit because you do. You give a shit about your pride, if not that poor SOB with a drug cartel after him. And I know you care about Presley's feelings, so stop acting like you don't."

Seth couldn't take much more of this, and Presley was headed back to him with two large coffees in her hands. He couldn't discuss this in front of her. Her wishes had been made clear.

"I'm hanging up. I'll call you when we land in Billings."

The city where Eric Harbaugh lived. They were not going to visit him or talk to him. They were going to mind their own business and stay out of it.

"Safe trip," Tanner said, signing off. Seth tucked the phone back into pocket and accepted the steaming hot paper cup from his wife.

"Who was on the phone?"

"Tanner, just updating me on the cartel investigation."

The java was surface of the sun hot and disturbingly dark. Just the way he liked it.

Presley's smile punched him in the gut. "Is it all set? Have they taken Eric into protective custody?"

She was calling him "Eric" like she knew him or that he was a friend. Presley was identifying far too closely with this guy. He could be a real asshole for all they knew. A jerk and a bastard.

Shrugging casually, he didn't want to have this conversation in an airport or on a plane.

"You know the government. Red tape and bureaucracy."

Her smiles quickly turned to a frown. "I hope they hurry. He could be dead before they get all the paperwork filled out."

"Hopefully the cartel wants money more than a dead body."

It was possible once they were home and Presley had her pregnant friend and a new business to worry about she'd forget all about the situation with Harbaugh.

And bison might sprout wings and fly over Yellowstone National Park.

There had to be a compromise. One that satisfied Presley

without them actually getting involved in someone else's problems. Dangerous problems. Now that she was out of jeopardy for the second time in her life he wasn't anxious for there to be a third.

Presley wasn't angry with Seth. Not truly. He was doing what he thought was the right thing to protect her and their family and for that she was grateful. He was a good man and a wonderful husband, even if he did snore like a tractor and played farting games with their son.

But right now she wasn't happy.

Seth had a point that she was turning Eric Harbaugh's situation into something far more personal than it needed to be. It was, however, kind of personal. His brother Danny had wanted to kill her and Seth, plus Eric thought they had the bank robbery money. They were involved whether Seth wanted to admit it or not. He wanted to walk away and go back to their lives as if nothing happened. She simply wasn't sure she could do that. People had helped her when Nora wanted her dead but no one was coming to this man's aid. They were going to let him die all because he'd had the bad luck to be born into the wrong family.

It wasn't fair, and although she'd long ago realized that life played favorites it didn't mean she had to like it. If anything, it made her want to even the playing field.

With Ben and Lulu with their grandparents and Fergus with Eliza and Alex, the house seemed eerily empty when she walked in. After being gone for almost four days, the rooms were stuffy and she opened the French doors off of the kitchen to let in some fresh air. She'd emptied the refrigerator before they left so she'd need to visit the supermarket if they wanted to eat.

Seth stood in the middle of the kitchen, leaning a hip against the island. "Are you going to talk to me?"

"I'm not mad."

"Are you sure? Because you act mad."

Opening the fridge, she made a mental list of everything she needed to get. Milk. Eggs. Juice. They were getting low on ketchup too and she couldn't run out. Ben was putting it on everything these days. He'd eat a ketchup sandwich if she let him.

"I'm not mad," she said again. "I'm just disappointed."

"In me."

Quietly closing the refrigerator, Presley reached for the pad and pencil on the counter to make the list.

"It's not your fault. You just don't understand."

An emotion crossed his features but it was so quick she couldn't identify it. Wasn't sure she even wanted to, frankly. Was it impatience? Probably. Seth liked his control and order and here she was again turning his world topsy-turvy. He'd said he liked it but one look at his face told a far different tale.

"I do understand, babe. I know you see yourself in this guy and I know you want to help him but even if we found the money he couldn't keep it. We'd have to give it back. The cartel would still be after him."

"I know."

She did know and she was trying desperately to figure some-thing else out. Some way to help him that Seth would approve of and support.

"I'd like to know what happened to all that money too," Seth went on. He talked quite a bit when she wouldn't. "Believe me, I've thought about that case for years and Tanner was right, it does bug me a little, but we looked for the cash and we never found it. It's gone. I'm sure of it."

Except he didn't sound sure, and she'd liked to know all that

Tanner had said. He was one of the few people in Seth's life that he listened to.

"I know, Seth. I'm not arguing." She poked a finger in his chest. "You're arguing. With yourself. Let me know who wins. In the meantime, I'm headed for the supermarket. I thought we'd have spaghetti for dinner."

Throwing up his hands, Seth was obviously exasperated. "I can't help him. There's nothing I can do for him."

Nothing made sense and that she understood. Her wanting to help Eric had nothing to do with logic and everything to do with emotion. This was her issue to deal with. Her past rearing its ugly head and making her crazy. She'd deal with this but right now she wasn't sure how.

Slipping her purse over her shoulder, she palmed the car keys. "I heard you the first time and I get it. Now I'm going to the store. Is there anything specific you want?"

"No. Yes. Ice cream. Any flavor."

When Seth Reilly started in on the ice cream he was well and truly pissed the hell off. She'd better get a whole gallon. Then later they could pretend the kids had eaten it even though they were hundreds of miles away.

Because she had to acknowledge that there was no easy answer. Not everything had a straightforward solution. Not everything could be solved with rainbows and puppy dogs. Sometimes the situation just sucked.

Presley couldn't save the world. Hell, she couldn't even save herself when it came down to it. She had to trust her husband. Hopefully Eric Harbaugh had someone he could trust too.

# CHAPTER NINETEEN

The Reilly household hadn't been the cheeriest place in the last few days. Presley had done her best to act like it was all just fine but Seth could see the strain in her eyes. She wanted to help Eric Harbaugh and she didn't know how. Neither did Seth. Until he'd had a crazy idea. It was out there and probably not even possible but it was worth a try. So he'd called his good friend and old Army buddy Evan Davis, ex-US Marshal. The man that had brought Presley to Seth in a sort of "unofficial" witness protection. That had been the beginning of...everything.

And now Evan was calling him so Seth ducked out of the back of the station. No one needed to know about what he was doing. He hadn't yet told Presley any details in case it all went awry after getting her hopes up. Honestly, it was a shot in the dark.

"Hey, Evan. Any news?"

At the rate the government worked Seth highly doubted it but he was an eternal optimist. At least that's what Presley said all the time.

"You are one lucky son of a bitch," Evan growled. "I had to call in every goddamn favor I was owed to do this. They now wish they'd never said that they'd do anything to thank me after I helped out Marisa as a dirty agent. But I think we have it done."

Seth was so dizzy from relief and happiness he had to lean on his truck. This was amazing fucking news. He'd never in a million years thought Evan would be able to pull this off.

"Harbaugh is going into witness protection then? That's great news."

A growl from Evan traveled clearly through the phone all the way from Florida. "He'll have to cooperate, Seth. Whenever they finally take down that cartel, whether it's next year or ten years from now, he'll have to cooperate with the authorities and whatever they want him to do. Make contact with the cartel, act as bait, whatever."

"I can't thank you enough, man. Presley is going to be thrilled. This was the only way I knew to help the poor bastard."

"Frankly he's not a high value witness, Seth, and his testimony would only be icing on the cake, but he does have some value because he has something the cartel wants. That means they'll take his calls and meet with him. That has value to the DEA and the prosecutor. Hopefully there will be far more valuable witnesses than Eric Harbaugh as well, but they conceded that they could use him to aid their case. Of course, an extortion charge is going to be small potatoes when the DEA gets done with these guys. I'm told they're trying to link the cartel to Danny Harbaugh's murder."

That didn't make sense. Why kill Harbaugh if he owed them money?

"I heard it was an accident. Meth labs aren't the most stable of environments and I'm betting these guys aren't chemistry majors."

Or they might be. Seth had watched *Breaking Bad* but that

was only television.

"Could be. I don't think it matters much to you or me. The cartel might have done it or someone could have gone rogue. Could be an accident, too. Who knows? It's just one more thing that they want to investigate."

"So what happens now?"

"The Marshals will pay him a visit," Evan replied. "Make him the offer. He doesn't have to take it but if he does they'll hustle him out of his current life right away. No delay. No time to ponder what he should do. I hope he's up for making the decision."

Seth had no idea but he'd done his part. The rest was up to Eric Harbaugh.

"If he says no then at least we tried. Listen, I can't thank you enough for this. I have to admit that I was worried too, not just Presley. This does kind of remind me of her situation. Are you sure it's okay that you turned in all your markers and made an end run around the DEA?"

"It's fine," Evan laughed. "And technically it was you that made the end run. You might want to call Jason Anderson so he doesn't hear about it from someone else. As for the markers, what am I going to need the US Marshal Service for? I'm a thriller author living in a semi-tropical paradise with the woman of my dreams. Life is good. Seriously, I'm glad I could help. This Eric guy was seriously fucked eight ways to Sunday. At least now he has a chance of survival. I'd say this was a good days work, my friend."

A much better one than just a few hours ago. It felt like a weight had been lifted from Seth's shoulders. He hadn't wanted to acknowledge the concern he'd felt for a man he'd never met and whose brother wanted to kill him.

The Presley Effect.

Now he could tell her the good news and maybe see the smile that had been missing since they'd left Las Vegas.

Presley's eyelids fluttered sleepily and she groaned softly, reaching over Seth for the alarm clock on the bedside table to quiet the chirping alarm. Too damn early for humans. She didn't mind mornings much, although she'd never been one of those people who hop out of bed with a smile on their face and a song on their lips. Those people creeped her out. But the time on the clock was five-fifteen. That wasn't even morning really. It was still dark out. Heck, the sun didn't even want to be awake yet. But Seth's shift was early and that meant she needed to get the coffee going and even maybe make him some breakfast.

Because he was her superhero. He'd pulled off the impossible and she still couldn't quite believe it. He'd used his contacts with the Marshal service and then Evan Davis had used his contacts at the prosecutor's office to pressure the DEA to use Eric Harbaugh in their case against the cartel. Consequently, Eric was going to be offered witness protection. When Seth had told her the news last night she'd been jubilant. Sometimes the good guys do make the world a little more equitable. At least now Eric had a chance when before he'd had basically none, unless he somehow managed to disappear on his own.

Next to her Seth stirred, stretching his long arms above his head before curving his body around hers so he was the big spoon and she was the little one. His cock pressed into her backside as he dropped a kiss on her shoulder.

"Morning, baby. Sorry I didn't hear the alarm first."

"I need to get up anyway. There's plenty to do at the shop."

Those questing fingers were playing with her nipples and making her squirm. Seth had more on his mind this morning than coffee and toast. "I'll come by and help when I get off duty."

His teeth bit down on her earlobe and one of his hands slid between her legs.

"How much is this help going to cost me, handsome?"

He pressed harder against her and she could almost feel the blood pumping through the veins of his cock. "For you, babe? Free of charge."

Pushing back with her bottom, she moaned as his fingers plucked the tips of her breasts into rock hard pebbles. "We don't have time."

Her voice came out breathless and not nearly as firm as she'd wanted it to.

"Sure we do. Plenty of time," he whispered in her ear, his breath warm on her cheek. Wrapped up in his arms like this so safe and toasty, Presley wasn't in any hurry to get out of bed. She'd rather stay here all day with Seth.

He'd have to skip breakfast and take his coffee on the road with him which he did quite a bit, so it wasn't a terrible hardship.

She made one more half-hearted attempt. "I was going to make you breakfast."

"I'm not hungry for food."

He would be afterward but she didn't have a chance to argue with him. Those mad-skilled fingers were rubbing insistent circles around her clit, making speech impossible. Her head fell back onto his shoulder and she closed her eyes in pure bliss – one of his hands working their magic on her nipple and the other between her thighs. She was close to exploding when he lifted her leg back and over his own so she was completely open to him before his cock slid into the hilt.

Both she and Seth gasped for breath as he pulled out and thrust in again. And again. With every stroke he rubbed her clit and it didn't take long for her to explode, stars behind her lids. It took a few more thrusts but then he grunted and buried his face in her hair as his body strained against hers. Eventually his muscles relaxed but his hold on Presley was just as tight.

"Good morning, honey."

The sun still wasn't up yet but in the Reilly household it was a good morning. And now that she and Seth were safe, there would be a whole lot more of them.

# CHAPTER TWENTY

S eth was obviously losing what was left of his sanity. He wasn't thinking clearly or logically and that's why he was here standing outside the front door of one Matt Ardell, who used to be Danny Harbaugh's cellmate, hoping to find out…what? If Danny had ever said where he hid the money? It was highly unlikely but here Seth was in a rundown apartment just outside of Billings, knocking on the door and hating himself for it.

The door swung open and a strikingly thin man with a shock of dark curly hair stood in the doorway. A scar dissected his left eyebrow and his knuckles and arms were covered with jailhouse ink. He looked to be around thirty but he was probably much younger. Seth had learned quickly that the criminal life and prison tended to age people faster than normal.

"What do you want?"

It wasn't the friendliest greeting but at least Ardell had answered the door. It was more than Seth had hoped for, frankly.

"Are you Matt Ardell?"

The man scowled and curled his lip. "Who wants to know?"

*I don't have time for this shit. I don't even want to be here. Not really.*

"I'm not a probation officer and I'm not collecting a debt or selling anything so you can relax."

"Good for you. Who are you?"

"My name is Sheriff Seth Reilly and I'd like to talk to you about your former cellmate Danny Harbaugh."

It was a gamble telling Matt his name but if Danny had behaved true to form it just might get him inside.

Matt laughed and grinned, a smug expression coming over his gaunt face. "Sheriff Seth Reilly, huh? I've heard about you but I never thought we'd meet. I'd always assumed Danny would take care of you the first day he set foot outside prison. Yet here you are. Alive and kicking. It's a surprise, really."

"He didn't get a chance." Just in case Matt hadn't heard the news. "Ended up dead in a meth lab explosion."

The other man blinked in surprise. "Danny's dead? I don't get the paper so I hadn't heard."

"Nobody told you?"

Matt's chin lifted. "I'm keeping my nose clean. I don't hang out with any of my old friends."

Was he making any new ones? Did he know anyone in that cartel? Seth was curious but he wasn't about to waste any time or questions on Matt. This was about Danny.

"Can we talk about Harbaugh?"

Matt shrugged and stepped back, letting Seth pass. "Seeing as how he's dead I guess he can't object, but it's going to cost you."

The inside of the apartment looked as bad as the outside. Maybe worse. The furnishings were sparse and had seen better days, including the small kitchen table in the corner that looked lopsided. Seth sat down on the edge of the faded flowered couch and went straight to the point.

"I'm here trying to get some information about Harbaugh

and you shared a cell with him for three years."

Matt sat in the old rocking chair and stretched out his legs. "Don't cops pay their informants? If I'm going to talk I need some sort of compensation."

Seth almost rammed the cocky little asshole against the wall to scare him but decided at the last minute that wasn't a good idea. Matt Ardell wasn't Seth's problem, Danny was. He needed to keep his eye on the ball and not get sidetracked.

Honey just might get more flies than beating the shit out Ardell. But if that didn't work...

Seth reached into his pocket and fished out a twenty, tossing it on the coffee table. Ardell reached for it and wadded it up in his fist.

"You want to know about Danny Harbaugh? I'll tell you about him. He was an asshole most of the time but a loyal one, you know what I mean? If you were his friend he stood by you. That's hard to find in the joint, ya' know."

It was a real bromance story. Danny was a Prince Charming. Matt? Not so much. It had only taken twenty bucks and he was talking.

"And he stood by you?"

"He sure as hell did and I stood by him. We were friends." Matt laughed and pointed to Seth. "That's how I knew about you. Danny fucking hated your guts."

"Because he thinks I killed his wife Lyndsey?"

"He knows you did."

Seth could tell Matt about the ballistics report but it wasn't the point of the visit.

"So he told you that he wanted me dead because I killed the woman he loved?"

Matt cackled and shook his head. "You don't get it, do you? You didn't take the woman Danny loved. He didn't love

Lyndsey. But she was his meal ticket and you took that away. She was the brains behind their entire operation. Danny was a two-bit criminal knocking over convenience stores for gambling and liquor money when he met Lyndsey. She was the one that taught him how to rob a bank, score the big money. He was nothing without her and when she died he knew he was heading back to the minor leagues. When he was ripping off gas stations he was nobody, but a bank robber? They're somebody."

The criminal hierarchy had always been something of a mystery to Seth but this kind of made sense. Anyone could rob a store but a bank was different. It made Danny look smarter.

"So he wanted to kill me because he blamed me for losing his ticket to the big time. Was there anyone he really did love?"

Matt leaned forward, his eyebrows waggling. "Danny had a couple of chicks on the side. Hot ones, too. I guess he probably liked or loved them. Kind of, anyway. I think he was good to them. He said he didn't hit them or nothing."

Romantic devil. What more could a woman ask for?

"Did he trust them?"

Matt shrugged. "Danny didn't trust anybody but Danny. You get a little paranoid in this business, man, and for good reason."

"But if he had to trust someone," Seth pressed. "Would he have trusted them? Would they have helped him if he was on the run from the law?"

"You'll have to ask them."

Seth pulled a small notebook and pen from his breast pocket and slid it closer to Matt. "I will if you can give me their names. Do you remember?"

At first the man hesitated but then relented, scratching out two names in the notebook, apparently deciding that Seth would get them one way or another.

"You didn't get these names from me."

"Hell, you and I have never even met. I've never heard of you in my life."

Matt grinned. "Exactly. Strangers."

"What else can you tell me about Danny?"

"He was a typical guy. He liked women and beer. He liked betting on sports but was lousy at it. That's what started him robbing stores."

Seth hadn't heard the gambling angle but it explained how Danny had gone in a much different direction than his brother Eric.

"Did he continue betting in the joint?" Seth assumed that he had. Addicts couldn't go without their fix. "Where did he get the money?"

That had Matt clamming up, the smile wiped from his face. "You ask too many questions. It's time for you to leave."

Not yet. Seth didn't budge from the couch.

"You were in for possession with the intention to distribute, correct?"

"It was a set up. I was just holding for a friend."

"I'm not your parole officer or your priest. I just want to know if Danny was involved with the cartel before or after he met you."

"I don't know what you're talking about."

"No wonder you were found guilty," Seth snorted. "You're a lousy liar. Now tell me how Danny got involved with the cartel and ended up owing them money."

Seth reached into his wallet and pulled out a second twenty dollar bill, tossing it on the table.

Matt was silent for awhile but Seth had been in way too many interrogations to lose patience. He simply sat quietly as well, waiting for Matt to break. People in general abhor a vacuum and seek to fill it with talking.

"He needed the money," Matt finally said, sighing heavily, reaching for the bill. "He'd lost big on the playoffs and he needed some cash. I introduced him to a buddy of mine and Danny started to do some deals but some of the merchandise was…misplaced…or stolen. Anyway, he owed them for it and he said he could get it when he got out. That he could get money on the outside plus he was planning on continuing to work for them. They didn't seem too worried about the cash as long as they had Danny doing their dirty work."

Now Seth was getting somewhere.

"He said he could get money on the outside? The bank robbery money? Is that what he was talking about?"

"I don't know." Matt shrugged helplessly. "Danny never said specifically but they kept him alive because he was working for them. I got out before he did so I don't know what happened after that. Are we done now?"

"One more question." Matt's jaw tightened but Seth wouldn't be deterred. "If you had to guess – and it can be a wild guess – but if you had to guess where Danny hid his money, where would it be?"

"Shit," Matt scoffed. "I don't know and I don't want to know. Knowing things is what gets you dead in this world, Sheriff. You ought to know that. It's better to be stupid and know nothing."

Then this guy should live forever.

"But Danny's already dead," Seth pointed out. "He can't hurt you. C'mon, he must have said something in three years. That's a long damn time."

"He never said where he put his money, but…"

"But," Seth prompted. "But what?"

"There was this place he liked to go, some fishing shack near Glistening Lake. He talked about it all the time, constantly. If he was going to hide anything I'm thinking it would be there."

That was pretty vague but still nowhere near where Seth had caught Danny. If the money was hidden there someone had to have done it for him.

"You don't know exactly where it is?"

"No, he only said that it was quiet and peaceful. That's it. That's two more questions."

Tucking the notebook and pencil back into his pocket, Seth nodded in agreement. "You're absolutely right. Thank you for your time."

They both stood and moved toward the door. "And we never met, right?"

"We never met," Seth replied. This hadn't been the waste of time he'd assumed it would be. "Never heard of you. Never met you. Complete and total strangers."

By the time Seth was driving back toward Harper, he had a smile on his face. Maybe it wasn't so crazy for him to be obsessed with where the money went because it just might still exist. Danny might have thought so. Seth needed to talk to the two girlfriends and see what they had to say and if they agreed with Matt.

Seth might be able to find that bank money and solve this mystery once and for all. It had only cost him forty bucks.

# CHAPTER TWENTY-ONE

Seth pulled into the mostly empty parking lot of the road-house. It was Sunday morning, overcast and cool despite the calendar saying that summer wasn't yet quite finished. It was the regular meeting of the sheriffs and Seth had a great deal to report. After talking to Matt yesterday he hadn't had a chance to bring his friends up to date.

The other men were already seated around a large table and Seth slid into his seat, bringing the conversation to grinding halt. All eyes turned to him, which had him wanting to bolt from the room. He never liked being the center of attention.

"What?"

Reed, newly back from following Seth's parents, Ben, and Lulu to Memphis, chuckled and popped open a soda can. "I think we all just wanted to see the luckiest son of a bitch in Montana. You went to Vegas to get away from a killer but he conveniently dies in an unrelated accident and you get to gamble and see shows for the rest of the weekend."

Seth and Presley had actually spent the majority of their time in bed.

"He wanted me dead," Seth replied. "That doesn't seem all

that lucky."

"It's lucky to me," Griffin declared. "You lead a charmed life."

Seth had a great life but he wouldn't go so far as to call it charmed. But he did feel like a lucky man just not for the reasons they were thinking.

Reaching for a soda from the center of the table, Seth quirked an eyebrow at Tanner and Dare.

"You two have been quiet. What do you think?"

Tanner stroked his chin and then smiled. "I think you could be called lucky."

"I think you're a pain in the ass," said a scowling Dare.

"You think everyone is a pain in the ass," Griffin pointed out with a smirk. "So that's not anything new or special."

"Well, they are," Dare muttered, taking a big drink from his coffee cup. "Everyone. All the time."

"I don't how Rayne puts up with you," Reed laughed. "She has the patience of a saint."

Just the mention of his pretty wife had Dare smiling. "She's no saint but she's not a pain in the ass, either."

"If she was you wouldn't tell her. She'd kick your ass," Griffin said. "Now are we going to get started? Jazz wants to go see a movie this afternoon."

Tanner pounded the table twice to start the meeting. "Sounds like a good idea to get started. Any new business?"

Seth raised his hand. "I do."

"Jesus, again? Who else is trying to kill you?" Reed asked.

Shaking his head, Seth gave Tanner a sheepish look. "No one that I know of. I'm actually looking into that original bank robbery with Danny and Lyndsey Harbaugh. You know the money was never recovered and we looked for a long time. I'm kind of...investigating the possibilities on that matter."

Tanner cleared his throat and it looked like he was trying not to laugh out loud. "I think that's a fine idea. Get some closure on the case and finally find out where Danny hid the cash."

Tanner probably wanted to say a whole hell of a lot more but to his credit he didn't. Although he did grin like a loon.

"That's what I was thinking," Seth said, fighting the urge to roll his eyes. "I'll admit this has bothered me for some time. So yesterday I went and talked to Harbaugh's former cellmate Matt Ardell. He had an interesting story to tell."

Seth quickly filled them in, handing over the names of the two girlfriends to Dare so he could check them out and perhaps find their current whereabouts.

"Are these their full names?" Dare asked, scribbling the information down into a notebook of his own.

"I don't know," Seth admitted. "I'm not even sure that Matt has their names right. He's a little strange. I just have my fingers crossed."

"And you don't have anything more on the fishing shack?" Griffin stood and strolled over to the coffee pot to refill his cup. "That's a pretty large area to check."

Dare was still making notes. "I can check the property records in the area but if he didn't own it then nothing is going to come up. Maybe a friend or family member? Does he have anyone besides his brother?"

Seth shook his head. "Not that I know of. Stan didn't mention anyone else that could pay Danny's debt off."

"Doesn't mean there isn't someone," Reed pointed out. "Just means that the cartel didn't know about them. Eric and Danny weren't hatched. They had to have had parents even if they've passed on. And those parents might have had siblings."

"I'll check," Dare said. "I didn't turn anything up before but I didn't dig all that deep. I do know the parents are dead but there might be a distant cousin out there."

Seth brought them up to date on the Eric Harbaugh situation and how Evan had pulled off a miracle. Surely by now he was in protective custody. Seth made a mental note to call his friend and get an update.

"I think Eric Harbaugh is a luckier man than you are," Griffin said. "His situation has certainly improved because of you."

"I hope so."

It certainly made Presley happy and Seth had to admit that it felt like he'd accomplished something here. He didn't always feel that way in law enforcement but this was one of the better days.

"So what are your next steps?" Tanner asked Seth as the meeting drew to a close. Reed had updated the group on a series of home invasions and Griffin had brought up a rash of car thefts that seemed to be focused on early model vehicles, probably for the parts.

Tanner and Seth exited the roadhouse, pulling on their jackets. It had started to rain while they were inside. "I'm going to try and talk to the two girlfriends and see what they know. If they can't help, I might go visit some of Lyndsey and Danny's neighbors. They might know where that shack is."

Tanner leaned against the bumper of Seth's truck. "Do you think that's where the money is?"

"It's a long shot," Seth admitted. "There's no way Danny could have hid it there himself. Not when I was chasing him. It's way too far out of the way from where I found him. But I suppose he could have given it to someone to hide there. The one thing that bugs me is that if the money is there why didn't he head straight for the shack when he was released from prison? As far as we know he never visited there in the week or so he was out."

"That we know of," Tanner repeated. "With a cartel after me I wouldn't have gone myself but sent someone I trusted. After all, they could have taken the money from the hiding place and killed Danny."

"No honor among thieves."

"Exactly, but I do think you're right. This is a long shot but I don't blame you for wanting to take a look. I would, too." Tanner slapped Seth on the back. "I wish you luck because I think you're going to need it. If the money was easy to find it wouldn't still be missing."

That was the crux of all of this. How did a sack of cash just disappear during a manhunt? Was it long gone and spent? Or had Danny managed the almost impossible and found someone he trusted to hide it?

So many questions and no answers. Typical day for a cop.

"Is there anything you want to tell me, Seth Reilly?"

Presley gave her husband an appraising look as she tapped her foot on the floor, waiting for his reply. He'd told her last night that he'd worked all day and that's why he couldn't help out at the coffee shop. But Deputy Hank had stopped by this morning to borrow a large party tray for his wife Alyssa. She was getting ready to have a birthday party for their son. Hank hadn't been there ten minutes before mentioning that Seth had taken the afternoon off yesterday. Presley had acted as if she'd known, but her husband had some explaining to do.

Frowning, Seth hung his jacket on the hook by the front door and then pulled off his boots. "I don't think so. Why?"

"Are you sure? Because it's better to just tell me than to let me find out on my own."

"Really, I don't have anything to tell you." Seth looked truly perplexed. "Is there some reason you think I do?"

"Hank stopped by this morning. He mentioned that you took yesterday afternoon off. Care to share about that?"

A look of relief crossed Seth's features. "Oh, that. It's no big deal, and I'm sorry I wasn't able to help yesterday. Are you mad?"

"*Oh, that,*" she mimicked. "I am not mad. I am suspicious. Do you remember that lovely talk we had in Vegas where we both agreed that we wouldn't keep things from each other? Does that ring a bell?"

Disappearing into the kitchen for a moment, he reappeared with two bottles of water in his hands. He handed one to her which she took gratefully. She'd been cleaning the house all morning because it wasn't often that Seth and both children were out of the house at the same time. She'd even managed to organize the play area.

"It does but I didn't think this was a big deal. I went to see Danny Harbaugh's former cellmate yesterday afternoon. I wanted to talk to him about where he thought Danny might hide the money."

Honestly, Presley hadn't had a clue as to why Seth hadn't told her about taking yesterday afternoon off. She's assumed it really wasn't a big deal but she didn't want them to go down a slippery slope and start not talking to each other again. About the important things, anyway. She didn't need to know that his indigestion was flaring up again, although if it did she'd remind him to take a Zantac or a Tums. He never remembered and then he'd be up in the middle of the night, wandering the house.

But in her wildest dreams she'd never thought the reason would be that he was visiting with Danny's cellmate. This was a shock.

"Seth, this is a big deal. When did you change your mind and decide to look for the money?"

He shrugged sheepishly. "In the last couple of days. Tanner's right. It's been bugging me for years and I'd like to find it." He held up a hand. "Not for Eric Harbaugh, but just for closure. I don't know how Danny ditched the money and made it so we couldn't find it."

Putting her hands on her hips, she sighed. "Of course, Tanner. You'll listen to him but not to your wife. I'm going to try not to be too hurt by that. And does he know that you're looking for the money?"

The color in Seth's cheeks told the tale. "I said something this morning at our meeting. I was going to tell you."

"Eventually."

"I swear I am not keeping secrets again," Seth groaned, falling back into his favorite chair, a brown leather recliner that had a perfect line of sight to the television. "It was just one of many things I did yesterday."

"I'll tell you what. I'm going to let this go. If…" She smiled, a little larceny in her soul. "If you take me dancing tonight. I want a night out on the town before the kids come back."

"Ah baby, not dancing," he protested but it was half-hearted. They were going. He just hadn't admitted it yet.

"You offered in Las Vegas," she reminded him. "So we can go tonight. It's a Sunday so there won't be a crowd."

"I was hoping for a crowd," Seth mumbled under his breath, "so that no one will notice how I dance."

"Invite your friends. Griffin dances worse than you do."

Seth's friend always looked like he'd been hit with a Taser on the dance floor.

"I'm going to tell Griffin what you said," Seth warned her with a grin. "But then I think he knows. I'll give them a call and see who can join us. It's last minute, though."

That's what made it so perfect. A little spontaneity never hurt anyone.

But now she had to figure out something to wear.

# CHAPTER TWENTY-TWO

Presley hadn't completely unpacked from Las Vegas yet so it only took a moment to find the little black dress she'd packed but hadn't had a chance to wear on vacation. She'd purchased it for the trip to Florida last year at the urging of Marion during a shopping trip in Billings.

"Every woman should have a cute black dress," Seth's mother had said when Presley had tried it on. "And that one is perfect. Dressy but not over the top. Perfect for almost any occasion."

It was fantastic and Presley felt like a million bucks in it. She loved the way the skirt swirled around her thighs and the neckline was low enough to show some cleavage but not so risqué as to give the waiter an eyeful. It was sexy and tasteful all at the same time.

She took extra time with her hair and makeup tonight, wearing a little more eyeshadow and mascara than she normally would. Her hair she styled half up and half down, letting some of the waves touch her shoulders but pulling the front back and away from her face with a gold barrette.

Slipping into her black high heels, she heard a whistle from the doorway. Seth. He looked dangerously yummy in his charcoal gray suit and blue tie. Maybe they should just stay in tonight. No…that's why she hadn't worn the dress in Vegas.

"Damn, you look good. I love your legs in those shoes. Keep them on later when we get home."

"Kinky bastard," she teased as she applied her lipstick. "It's a good thing Ben and Lulu can't hear you talk like that."

"They wouldn't know what it meant."

"I just don't want to be the reason they seek therapy as an adult."

Presley tucked her lipstick tube into her tiny black purse and smoothed down her hair one last time.

Harper didn't have much in the way of fine dining so they ended up in Valley Station, Dare and Rayne's town. There was a pretty decent steakhouse there, and if there was one thing the men were always enthusiastic for it was an oversized grilled piece of meat and a baked potato. Maybe a cold beer to wash it all down too.

Not only was Dare and Rayne meeting them for dinner, so was Reed and his author wife Kaylee. Presley rarely found opportunities to spend time with the girls so tonight was going to be fun. Rayne especially was pretty wild when she wanted to be, although most of the time she was quite sedate. She looked badass with her tattoos, piercings, and pink streak in her short black hair but she was actually one of the sweetest people Presley had ever met. But wow, she could put away some tequila. They'd stayed out all night at her bachelorette party and then nursed their hangovers all the next day.

Holding the door open for Presley, Seth ushered his wife into the dimly lit restaurant. Reed, Kaylee, Dare, and Rayne were already seated.

Presley opened her mouth to apologize but Rayne held up

her hand in a stop motion. "You aren't late. You are right on time. We just got here and these two..." She pointed to Reed and Kaylee. "Were a little early."

Kaylee, a cute brunette with an infectious smile just shrugged. "What can I say? I was anxious to get here. I've been working on a book and I don't think I've left the house in days, plus the cupboards were bare. We're starving, too."

Reed, a handsome dark-haired man with a quiet way about him, nodded in agreement. "We've been living on canned soup and frozen pizza for days. I can't wait to cut into a juicy steak."

Settling into her chair, Presley wanted to thank him for what he'd done for her and Seth.

"Reed, I want to say thank you again for traveling with my parents and the kids. You dropped everything to do that and I'm so grateful." She turned to Kaylee. "And I want to thank you too because you had to do without him for a few days while he was gone. So thank you so much. I can't tell you how much better it made me feel that he was watching over them."

Kayla waved away her thanks as her husband flushed, his cheeks pink. "Don't even worry about it. I kind of like the quiet every now and then so I can work."

"I was happy to help," Reed said with a smile. "I'm just glad that nothing happened."

"You must have been going crazy not being able to be with Ben and Lulu," Kaylee said. "I can't even imagine how hard that must have been. You were so strong and brave."

Presley hadn't felt that way but she didn't want to wallow in what had been a nightmare of a few days. She still missed her children but now she could be happy that they were having an adventure with their grandparents. She talked to them every day on Skype or the phone and they were having the time of their lives. And learning lots of new Elvis songs. She was sure there would be a concert when Ben and Lulu returned home.

"Tell me about the book you're writing," Presley invited, anxious to change the subject. "When will it be out?"

The conversation was as good as the meal, although Rayne seemed rather quiet and subdued, not laughing as much as everyone else. Dare did his usual scowling so it was hard to tell his emotional state on any given day and tonight was no exception. By the time their dessert order was taken Presley had a feeling that Rayne and Dare might be in a tad of a domestic tiff. It had happened to Presley and Seth, of course, as it did most couples at one time or another. They'd made plans to have dinner with Marion and George and then ended up snarling at each other over fried chicken. The fight had been stupid because she couldn't even remember what it was about but at the time it had seemed damned important.

Pushing back her chair, Presley excused herself. "I'll be right back."

Rayne jumped up immediately. "I'll go with you. I need to powder my nose."

All eyes turned to Kaylee who also stood, clutching her purse to her chest. "I guess I might as well...um...I'll go, too."

Three women and six legs hurried to the ladies' room. Presley had never been one for a group trip to the bathroom but she was beginning to see the reasons behind them. Clearly Rayne wanted to talk.

"I'm going to kill him," the tiny woman growled when the door closed behind them. "Slowly and painfully. I can do it, too. He's a heavy sleeper."

A smile playing around Kaylee's lips, she propped her purse on one of the sinks and pulled out her lipstick. "We can call Ava and get some ideas of how to do it from her. She's a mystery writer and knows about fifty ways to kill someone and make it look like the family cat did it."

"Let me guess," Presley said, checking her hair in the mirror. "You and Dare had an argument right before coming to dinner."

Rayne smacked her handbag down on the side of the sink. "He actually had the nerve to say that we had more sex before Cherish was born. Can you believe that? I let him know just why we weren't having as much sex. Asshole."

Kaylee's brows shot up. "Was he complaining or just sort of making a casual observation?"

"A little of both, I think. I said how nice it was that we were getting a night out on the town while my sister watches the baby. That's it. That's all I said. Then he says that a lot has changed since Cherish was born. I don't cook as much, we don't go out as much, and we don't have sex as much. I just stood there for the longest time not really believing that those words came out of my husband's mouth. I mean...he was the one that pushed to have a baby right away. He couldn't wait, he was so excited."

"Is he not excited and happy now?" Presley asked carefully.

Sighing heavily, Rayne shoulders slumped. "He loves Cherish so much. I know he does. But I'm not sure he still loves me."

Presley had a few painful memories of those days after Ben was born. How she didn't feel sexy and it was hard to communicate that to Seth. He thought it was about him and it had made things awkward.

Presley and Kaylee's eyes met over Rayne's head.

"I'm sure he still loves you," Kaylee replied. "Have you talked to him about it?"

"All we do is argue." Rayne wiped a tear from her cheek. "I need more of Dare's help but I don't know how to ask him. I'm exhausted every single hour of every single day. Some days I'm so tired I'm almost numb. I could smack myself in the head with a hammer and I don't think I'd feel it. I'm trying to take care of my daughter, run the tattoo shop, and be a wife too. Honestly, I don't think I'm doing any of those things very well. I know motherhood isn't supposed to be easy but is it supposed to be this hard? I'm failing here and I don't know how to stop the spiral down."

The crippling doubt that she was a decent mother was also a familiar refrain. Presley had had her share and even now she often wondered if she was doing the right things for her children. As she'd said earlier to Seth, she didn't want to be the reason they sought counseling when they grew up.

"You're a wonderful mother," Presley said. "Babies aren't complicated. They need food, love, and clean diapers. I know you give her everything she needs because I've seen you with Cherish. You're doing a great job."

There ought to be cheerleader services for new parents because they needed all the positive reinforcement they could get. If she hadn't been so busy with her new business she would have realized that Rayne would be going through this.

More tears. "I'm a terrible mother. I don't spend enough time with her. I work too much. She's going to hate me."

"She is not going to hate you," Kaylee said, wrapping an arm around Rayne. "You're her mother and she's going to love you. I know that. But if you need help you have to ask Dare for it somehow. As much as we'd like it to happen, these men can't read our minds."

Rayne threw her hands up in the air. "Can't he see it? Jesus, the house is a mess, I barely shower, there's no dinner being cooked, and I'm falling asleep on my feet. Can't he see that I'm overwhelmed? Before we came here tonight he literally tripped over the piles of dirty laundry."

"So when he said what he did about the sex, what did you say?" Presley asked.

"I just—I just lost it. Everything that I'd been keeping locked up inside of me bubbled over and I let him have it with both barrels. I told him he was a selfish dick who never helped me around the house and that's why he wasn't getting laid as much. Because he's a jerk. I can't believe I married such a dumbass."

That must have gone over well. Not that Presley and Seth hadn't had the very same argument. They had. But luckily, she'd exploded much earlier. Clearly Rayne had been holding on to this way too long. Her shoulders were now shaking with the force of her sobs.

What Rayne truly needed was a long hot bath, a glass of wine, and a good night's sleep. In fact, she needed several of them. In a row. Sleep deprivation was making this situation look far worse than it actually was. But that didn't mean it wasn't kind of awful. Rayne and Dare were a great couple together and they might just need a little nudge in the right direction to make up. The first thing Rayne needed to do was get everything off of her chest. All of her complaints – big and small. She'd feel better afterward. Then they could work on figuring out a way to tell Dare he needed to step up and help more.

Digging a tissue out of her purse, Presley dabbed Rayne's wet cheeks. "Men are jerks but they're our jerks. You can fix this. Seth and I have had this argument many times."

Rayne's eyes widened in horror and her mouth fell open. "Oh my God, you mean I'm going to have to tell him more than once?"

Well…yes.

# CHAPTER TWENTY-THREE

B ack at the table, Reed shook his head in disbelief. "Dude, you are so fucked. You'll be surfing the sofa for months. Don't you know when to shut the hell up?"

Apparently not. Seth had trouble hiding his laughter when the story of why Dare and his wife were barely speaking to one another came out. Dare had a righteous anger going that was completely misplaced and the poor bastard was going to have to apologize. Probably more than once.

Dare pointed to his chest. "She was yelling at me. She was the one who lost her temper. I was just standing there. It was totally unprovoked."

Seth knew better. There was nothing his friend Dare liked more than a good argument where he had an excuse to scowl and be grouchy.

"And you were just standing there like a choir boy," Seth taunted. "Totally angelic and pure as the driven snow. Fuck no, you complained about sex and anytime in the first year of a baby's life you simply cannot do that. Unless you were looking for a fight. Then that's different."

Dare gave him an exasperated look. "But it's true. We are

having less sex, and she doesn't cook as much. I'm not lying."

Reed rolled his eyes. "Even I know that it doesn't matter whether it's true. That's not the point."

"How is it not the point?" Dare asked. "I said the truth and then she came back at me with a bunch of complaints. I do help around the house."

Seth had vague memories of what he used to consider "helping" and how having two children had changed his perspective. "Okay, when was the last time you did a load of laundry?"

"Two weeks ago," Dare said with a smug smile. "See? I've helped."

Two weeks ago? Dare was delusional. With a new baby, there was laundry to be done almost every day.

Reed's brow quirked up. "Did you do the load all the way through to the folding or did you just throw it in the washer with some soap and let Rayne take care of it from there?"

Dare's smiled faltered. "I can't fold clothes very well, especially those tiny baby pajamas with the feet in them."

"Then you better learn," Seth replied firmly. "Because ignorance of a skill is no excuse and I'm sure you managed to fold your own clothes before you got married. How about diapers? Do you change diapers?"

"Of course I do. I changed one tonight while Rayne put on her makeup."

That was something.

"In the middle of the night when Cherish is crying do you get out of bed at least half of the time?"

"Rayne is breastfeeding."

Poor dumb bastard. No wonder Rayne was pissed. But it made sense in a way. If Dare's sister Sophie were still living with them this wouldn't have happened but she was in college now, so he didn't have anyone to straighten his ass out.

"You could get up and go get Cherish," Seth suggested. "Bring her into Rayne. Maybe go get her some water or a snack if she's hungry. You know, just be part of it and supportive."

"Why?"

Reed cuffed Dare on the head. "You're as stupid as a bag of hammers. Because it would make her feel more appreciated."

Dare growled and bared his teeth but no one paid him any mind. "Then both of us get a lousy night's sleep. How is that helpful?"

Seth realized he was going to have to draw Dare a map. "You need to listen to me very carefully. Rayne needs your help. She's exhausted trying to take care of everything and frankly, your sexual needs aren't even on the list. If you want to have more sex then step the fuck up and give her a hand. That woman needs some uninterrupted sleep. Have Rayne freeze some milk so you can give it to Cherish in a bottle from time to time, especially at night. Do the damn laundry. Fix dinner even if it's only a frozen pizza or bring home takeout. Stop acting like a child and be a grownup. You're the parent now and I will tell you that you two need to work together and help each other out. God help you if you don't because you don't want to turn on each other when the kid becomes a toddler. That's going to make this time in your life look easy."

From the expression on Dare's face this was news he hadn't known.

"I do want to help her out but nothing I do is ever good enough so I stopped offering." Dare's shoulder's sagged in defeat. "When Cherish first came home I offered to give her a bottle but Rayne said no bottles. Then I offered to take her for a walk around the block in her stroller, Rayne said it was too cold. Then it was too hot. Or Cherish shouldn't be around people because they had germs. Or I wasn't holding her right and was going to drop her. I wasn't going to drop my daughter. Nothing I do is right and she knows more about babies than I do. I figured I'd better do what she said."

"What she says and what she feels is too different things. Presley felt the same urge to be supermom. Sometimes you have to wrest the baby out of their arms and send them to bed to get some sleep. You're the dad and you get to make decisions too. As long as you're not feeding your daughter lead paint and giving her poisonous snakes as pets it should be okay. Ben and Lulu love it when I take them out and it gives Presley some peace and quiet."

Reed rubbed the back of his neck. "Just whatever you do, don't complain about the lack of sex. Just don't. Not even if you have flowers in one hand and a gourmet meal cooked in the other."

Seth chuckled as he remembered the early days of parenthood. "The idea of what is romantic changes a little bit. At least it did for me and Presley. She didn't want me to come home with champagne and chocolates. She didn't care about going out for fancy dinners or expensive jewelry. It was the little things that became romantic. Shoulder and foot rubs when she was pregnant and achy. Changing the poop-filled diaper instead of pretending you didn't smell it. And don't say that you haven't done that because we all have. Just find ways to help her. Clean the litter box for that crazy cat that looks like Kirk Douglas. What's his name...Spartacus? And don't forget to tell her she's beautiful. When was the last time you did that?"

"Tonight," Dare replied with a huff of impatience. "When I told her I wanted to have sex that means she's gorgeous."

Reed shook his head in amazement. "I have no idea how you ever managed to get a woman to fall in love with you. None."

"You know I love Rayne more than anything," Dare said, his

voice soft. "She and Cherish are everything to me but I'm not always the most…communicative person."

Both Seth and Reed laughed at the understatement.

"You don't say," Seth drawled. "Hard to believe."

"I just don't understand how we got so off track," Dare said. "Everything was great and then suddenly it wasn't."

Seth nodded. "Babies will do that. But you and Rayne can fix this. Just apologize."

Dare didn't have a chance to say whether he was going to or not as the three women returned from their own meeting in the ladies' room. Rayne's eyes looked slightly red and puffy but she was wearing a smile that hadn't been there twenty minutes ago. That was a good sign.

An even better sign was the way Rayne and Dare were looking at each other. Dare was a grouchy, scowling son of a bitch who hated just about everything and everyone. But his wife and child. He was looking at Rayne like she was the most perfect person on earth.

The way Seth looked at Presley.

Rayne's hand inched out and grabbed her husband's. "I'm so—"

"No," Dare said, shaking his head. "I'm sorry, angel. Really sorry."

"I'm sorry too, my big grouchy bear. I'm just so tired these days."

They were so going to bust Dare's balls about the "big grouchy bear" nickname. But not tonight.

There was more nuzzling and kisses, plus promises from Dare that he was going to be more help from now on which Seth believed. Dare and Rayne were going to work this out.

The vibrations from his jacket pocket pulled his attention from his friends and onto his phone.

*Evan.*

"How's sunny Florida? We had a nice cool day here."

"It's hotter than hell but I'm not calling to complain. There's been a development I thought you might be interested in."

Seth placed his hand over his other ear, blocking out the noise from the restaurant, so he could give Evan his full attention. "I'm listening."

"Eric Harbaugh has disappeared from witness protection sometime in the early morning hours. He slipped out under the cover of darkness and so far they haven't been able to find him. He might not be so innocent after all, my friend."

Presley pulled one of Seth's old t-shirts over her head. He'd told her about Eric Harbaugh only moments ago while she was brushing her teeth and she still wasn't sure how she was supposed to feel and respond.

"He ran away?" she finally asked, trying to grasp the stupidity of Eric's action. After Seth and Evan had gone out on limb for him he'd thrown his chance at survival away.

"He did," Seth confirmed, sliding into bed and flipping on the television. "Out of a window in the wee hours of the morning. I guess he'd rather take his chances on his own, which is dumb as hell but it's a free country. People can be as stupid as they want to be. And often do."

"Now Evan thinks that Eric might not be naive and innocent after all?"

"It's a suspicious move." Seth shrugged and clicked through the channels, landing on a news network. "I think he's probably more scared than anything and he bolted. Maybe he didn't think witness protection would work. Only he knows and he didn't leave a note filled with his thoughts."

Hopping into bed next to her husband, she settled down and picked up the remote. The news was depressing.

"Maybe he finally figured out where the money is."

From Presley's perspective that was the only explanation that made any sense, but it made her wonder how he might have done it.

"He's still going to get his ass killed," Seth scoffed. "Does he honestly think that he's going to give the bad guys the cash and they're going to let him walk away and back to his life? That's a fantasy. These guys don't leave witnesses."

"Could we–"

"No," Seth interrupted. "We tried to help him and he blew us off. I'm done with Eric Harbaugh."

Presley found a movie on television she hadn't seen in a long time, and she was far too keyed up to sleep. "I hope he really has found the money. For his own safety, of course, not because I don't want you to find it and give it back."

Seth frowned at her movie choice but didn't say anything, apparently deciding it wasn't worth the debate. "If he has a lick of sense – which I haven't seen evidence of – he'll use the money and completely disappear. Leave the country and change his name. Start a whole new, very low profile life in Portugal."

"Why Portugal?"

"Do you know anyone who travels to Portugal? But it's really beautiful there. I saw it on the Travel Channel."

"Airplanes travel to Portugal every day," Presley said as patiently as possible. "I'm sure lots of people travel there."

"I bet no one Eric Harbaugh knows has been there."

Sometimes marriage was strange as hell and right now was one of those moments. She was sure she hadn't had conversations like this with anyone else on the planet.

"You might have a point." She snuggled up to Seth, resting

her head on his shoulder. "But there's just one flaw in your plan for Eric to find the money and fly off to a foreign country so he can live happily ever after."

"What's that?"

"You're looking for the money too, and I'd bet on you every day of the week to find it first."

Chuckling, Seth ran his fingers through her hair. "You're good for my ego, baby, but if Harbaugh knows where it is then he's got a head start on me. Remember I wasn't able to find it last time."

"But you will this time," she said confidently. "You're going to talk to the girlfriends tomorrow, right? I bet they know something."

"I hope so but it could be a complete waste of time."

Presley traced circles on Seth's bare chest with her fingernail. "You know...that kitchen and bathroom tile place is out that way. We could talk to the girlfriends and then stop and look at tile for the master bath. You've been promising to replace it and it's on the list."

"We?" Seth flipped her over so she was on her back, his fingers tickling her ribs. She giggled and batted at his hands ineffectually. "What's all this about you going, too?"

"Stop it." She slapped at his arm and kicked her legs. "Stop it, it tickles."

"It's supposed to."

He did stop, but he didn't back off, instead hovering on top of her. She lifted her leg and rubbed her thigh against his hard cock. Her husband. Always ready no matter what. They might as well. She was wide awake and sleep was far away.

"Seriously, I want to go. You never let me help with the police work because it's official business. But this isn't. It's completely unofficial."

Seth rolled his eyes before dipping his head down and nipping at her exposed shoulder where the t-shirt was askew. He was trying to distract her and doing a decent job of it. Her entire body was on red alert.

"I don't take you because it's dangerous."

He began to press his body to hers but her hands came up to press back on his chest. Not yet. She had more to say.

"Are you expecting tomorrow to be dangerous?"

"If I say no and allow you to go will you shut up and let me kiss you?"

Giggling, she reached down and began to wriggle out of her t-shirt. She shouldn't have even bothered putting it on in the first place.

"Yes."

*This is much better than the movie.*

# CHAPTER TWENTY-FOUR

The day was warm but rainy when Seth and Presley drove to Corville the next morning to meet with one of Danny Harbaugh's girlfriends, Brittany Smithers. According to the little information Dare had been able to dig up, she was single with no children and worked as a legal secretary but had recently been laid off from her job. Hopefully they would find her at home.

"What are we going to say?"

Seth gave her a sideways glance. "You're not going to say anything. Let me do the talking."

Right. Like that was going to happen. He knew better than that.

"You know, it might help to have me talk to her a little. She might open up to a woman more easily than to a man, especially when it comes to relationships."

"Maybe," Seth grunted. "We'll see."

Now he was just being a jerk.

"You know that I can talk to people and get them to say anything. It drives you crazy most of the time but now it could be a real benefit to us."

His lips twisted in resignation. "I guess you're right. You do have that way about you. She'll probably tell you her whole life story, including her bank balance and social security number."

Presley smiled in triumph. "I'll try to keep her focused on Danny. So let's review what you hope to find out."

The rest of the drive didn't take long but they'd gone over the information that Seth needed to know. Mainly he wanted to ask if Danny had ever talked about any favorite places or about the fishing shack. They might even want to ask outright if she knew where the money was or what had happened to it. With any luck though, Brittany would just start talking and they'd get what they wanted without having to try.

"Are you ready? I'll let you do the talking. Let's hope she opens up to you."

They climbed out of the truck and walked up to the front door along the concrete path. Seth knocked and they both waited, holding their breath with hope that she was home. They certainly hadn't called ahead and given her a chance to tell them not to bother to come.

No answer. Seth knocked again, this time a little firmer but instead of Brittany's door opening the neighbor to the right stuck their head out of their door. The woman was in her sixties maybe, with short gray hair and bright blue eyes.

"Are you looking for Brittany? Are you friends of hers?"

Taking a deep breath, Presley plunged in. "Hi, I'm Presley and this is my husband Seth. We're from over in Harper and we were hoping to see Brittany today. Do you know where she is?"

The older woman smiled and stepped out of the door a little farther. Presley could hear the television in the background. "I'm Alice. Brittany is picking up a few shifts at the Corville Skillet. It's down on Maple just off of First. They make excellent pancakes."

"Thank you, Alice." Presley smiled and waved her thanks.

"We appreciate that and those pancakes sound delicious."

It was cold so Alice didn't linger, popping back into her apartment. "You're welcome. The hash browns are good too."

Presley looked up at Seth. "Are you hungry?"

They'd already eaten breakfast but her husband had a big appetite and could probably easily put away another.

"I could eat."

That was a yes. With only a few wrong turns they found the Corville Skillet, a gray building with a large sign out front with yes, a cast-iron skillet on it. There were several cars and trucks in the parking lot but the restaurant had empty tables. The hostess who greeted them had no problem seating them in Brittany's section.

"So what's the plan?" Presley asked, her gaze darting around the restaurant. Which young woman was Brittany?

"To eat," Seth replied. "If your past is any predictor of the future, she'll be telling you her life story before your eggs get cold."

"I'm not ordering eggs."

She did, however, like the sound of the homemade cinnamon roll. This was becoming a habit.

"Hello, I'm Brittany and I'm going to be taking care of you today. Would you like to start out with some coffee or juice?"

Brittany was of average height but she was an extremely attractive woman with dark hair, currently pulled back in a ponytail, and large brown eyes. What had a pretty girl like this been doing with a loser like Danny Harbaugh?

He must have been charming. Ick.

"Coffee for me," Presley replied with a friendly smile.

"Me too," Seth said.

Brittany made a note on her order pad. "Are you ready to order or do you need more time?"

Time to see if Brittany was a talker. "Is the cinnamon roll good?"

The woman pressed her hand to her heart and sighed. "To die for. Huge, too. They make them homemade every morning."

"That's sounds perfect. I'll have that." She nudged Seth across the table. "I might even let you have a bite."

Seth gathered up both their menus and set them on the edge of the table. "No, you won't. Now I'd like the eggs, bacon, and toast platter. Eggs over easy."

Because the only way Presley could make them was scrambled. No matter how hard she tried. So whenever Seth went out for breakfast he ordered his eggs over easy.

"White or wheat?"

"Wheat," Seth answered. "And a glass of orange juice. Small."

"Got it," Brittany said cheerily. "I'll put in your order and bring your coffee and juice."

The woman bustled away and disappeared into the kitchen, leaving Seth and Presley at the table wondering how to talk to her. She seemed happy and nice and honestly, Presley was loath to bring up Danny. If Brittany still loved him she was going to be upset that he was dead and if she hated him she was going to be upset just talking about him. They couldn't win either way.

"She looks like she's having a good day," Presley said glumly. "We're going to ruin it."

"Maybe not. Maybe she doesn't care about him anymore. She could have forgotten all about him. He's probably a distant memory by now."

Maybe, but Presley remembered every loser she'd ever dated whether she wanted to or not. There was a way they clung to the dark corners of the mind, skulking around and waiting to pounce at the worst possible moment.

Not sure how to engage the younger woman, Presley ate the delicious cinnamon roll when it was placed in front of her while simultaneously watching Brittany as she worked. She appeared to be friendly and efficient, smiling and joking with the customers. Presley could see why Danny would have found her attractive.

Seth wiped his mouth with his paper napkin and patted his stomach. "We're done and we haven't been able to talk to her at all. Frankly, honey, you're losing your touch because she hadn't tried to make you her best friend forever."

"Maybe I'm putting out a vibe," Presley said. "And she's running away from the desperation. This isn't a talent I have actual control of, you know. Now smile because she's coming over to the table again."

Brittany slid the check next to Seth's plate. "You can pay the cashier by the door. Thank you for coming in today and I hope you come back. My shift is finished but if you need anything else Kathy can help you. Thanks again."

Seth and Presley thanked Brittany and then practically fell all over themselves to pay the check and get outside when she disappeared into the back kitchen. They needed to talk to her before she got away. Holding jackets over their heads to shield them from the rain, they caught up with her behind the building where Brittany was unlocking a late model Honda Accord.

"Brittany," Presley called causing the woman to turn around. "Can you wait a second?"

"Uh, I guess." The waitress frowned but she didn't try to hurry away. "Is something wrong?"

Presley was breathing a little heavy and the rain was drizzling down her face.

"No, there's nothing wrong. Seth and I were just hoping we could talk to you."

Shit, that didn't help. If anything, Brittany's gaze nervously darted between them as if waiting to be kidnapped and sold into human trafficking.

Seth tried to be reassuring, flashing his badge. "It's nothing you need to fear, ma'am. We're just here looking for some information about Danny Harbaugh."

Rolling her eyes and slumping against the vehicle, Brittany groaned. "You're cops, huh? That's not a surprise. You want to know about Danny? I'll tell you what I tell everyone. He was a no-good, lousy liar who wouldn't know the truth if it slapped him in the face. He still owes me three hundred bucks but I doubt he'll ever pay it now that he's behind bars. Too bad you didn't put him there before I met him. Would have saved me a lot of heartache and trouble."

"Danny is dead," Presley said quietly. "He died in a meth lab explosion not long after being released from prison."

The words didn't appear to have any effect on Brittany Smithers. "If you're waiting for me to cry, you're shit out of luck. He made his own trouble and it was only a matter of time before karma caught up with him. I got sucked in by his charm because I was young but I'm a lot smarter now." The young woman sighed and her gaze fell to the ground. "Listen, I'm not sure what you want me to say about Danny but I got nothing good. He was cheating on me and his wife with other women, and he never had two nickels to rub together because he was always gambling and losing. That pretty much sums up Danny. A big old loser. Good riddance."

Presley shuffled uncomfortably on her feet. Clearly they'd brought up a sensitive subject.

"So you knew he was married?"

Brittany shrugged. "Not at first but eventually. He said she didn't understand him. I was young and didn't know that was the oldest excuse in the book. I do now."

"Did you know he and his wife were robbing banks?"

"I did after he was caught."

"Were you surprised?" Seth asked. "Did he talk about the bank jobs?"

Brittany shook her head. "No way. If he had I would have expected him to pay for something every now and then, even if it was just a cheeseburger. After our first few dates, he never had a dime and believe me, I checked his wallet when he wasn't looking. It was empty. Kind of like his soul."

Might as well just plunge in and take a chance.

"The money from his last bank heist went missing," Presley explained. "Somewhere between the bank and when Seth apprehended him."

Brittany looked at Seth with new respect. "You're the cop that sent him to prison? Good for you. As for the money, do you think I have it? Do I look like I have money? Believe me, if I did I wouldn't be waiting tables in this dump. I wouldn't have lost my house either when I got laid off."

"We don't think you have it," Seth replied with a slight smile. "But did Danny ever mention anywhere that was important to him? Anywhere that he might have hid the cash? Or maybe there was a person he was especially close to that might have helped him?"

"Danny only talked about two things – bets he was going to place and that stupid fishing cabin. That's it. He didn't read, he didn't keep up with current events, he didn't even like to go to the movies. He watched sports and placed bets on the games. When he wasn't doing that he'd disappear for days at a time at that stupid cabin. Is that all you wanted to know? It's raining harder."

It was pouring and Presley was soaked. Seth thanked the woman for her time and they headed back to the front of the building and the blessed shelter of the truck. Climbing into the passenger seat, she clipped on her seatbelt. The day had only begun. Next stop was girlfriend number two and if Brittany was any indication the second one wouldn't have anything nice to say about Danny Harbaugh.

One thing though was clear. They needed to find that fishing cabin.

# CHAPTER TWENTY-FIVE

Girlfriend numbers two's life was in stark contrast to Brittany Smithers. Alexa Lansford was clearly living the high life if her home was any indication. The house could honestly be called a mansion and the cars parked in front of it were decidedly expensive and European. It looked like Danny had diverse tastes when it came to females.

"I'd say she might have the money but two hundred thousand would be a drop in the bucket here," Presley said as they exited the truck. "That's probably just what they pay the gardener."

"This is big money," Seth agreed, eyeing the impressive facade. "I doubt a hundred grand would be anything that would excite them but you never know. Maybe she wanted it for a shopping trip."

Presley gave him a sour look. "Not all women like to shop. Stop stereotyping."

"Fine, maybe she wanted to give it to widows and orphans. And puppies."

Huffing, Presley led the way to the front door. "You're so cynical sometimes."

"That's what you love about me. Now we're just going to tell the truth, right? Just lay it all on the line?"

He and Presley had gone back and forth during the drive here but he didn't like subterfuge if he could help it. Better to be up front and honest from the first moment. If Alexa Lansford didn't want to talk to them that was certainly her right.

But he hoped that she would.

Presley rang the doorbell and waited, her more patiently than Seth. After talking to Brittany he was more anxious than ever to talk to Lansford. Perhaps she knew where the fishing cabin was located. It was a long shot. No, make that a long-long shot because Danny would have needed help to get the money to the cabin, but it was worth a look. It was their only lead in a vast sea of nothingness. If they could find it.

The door opened and a pretty woman in her mid-thirties stood there. Auburn hair, green eyes, nice figure. If this was Alexa, Danny had good taste and clearly over-achieved with women.

"Can I help you?"

She probably thought they were selling something or wanted to talk about politics or religion. He pulled his badge out of his pocket and held it up for her inspection. It tended to add credibility in situations like this.

"Hello, I'm Sheriff Seth Reilly from Harper and this is my wife Presley. Are you Alexa Lansford?"

She nodded, puzzlement in her eyes. "I am."

"We were hoping you might have a moment to talk to us…about Danny Harbaugh."

The woman glanced nervously over her shoulder.

"My husband is at work so I suppose it would be okay. Is Danny in trouble again?"

Seth didn't answer and neither did Presley as they entered

the palatial home, all dark oak and marble floors. Alexa led them to a sitting room off the foyer, waving toward a couch where they could sit down.

She remained standing, hovering uncertainly. "Can I get you anything...?"

Seth shook his head. "We're fine. We'd just like to talk to you for a few minutes, if that's okay."

Alexa smiled and perched on the edge of a chair across from them, her hands folded neatly in her lap. "I haven't heard Danny's name in years. Was he arrested again?"

Seth and Presley exchanged a worried glance. Alexa seemed much more concerned about Danny's well-being than Brittany had. But he'd decided to tell the truth.

"Actually, Danny is dead," Seth replied gently. "Not long ago. About a week."

Alexa's eyes widened and her hand flew to her mouth in shock. "Oh my God. What happened?"

"An explosion," Presley said. "It was an accident. When was the last time you saw or heard from Danny?"

Eyes bright with tears, Alexa took a moment before answering. "It's been years. Even before he was arrested and sent to prison. We broke up..."

Alexa's voice dropped and she seemed to have trouble finishing her thought.

"And?" Presley prompted. "You and Danny ended things?"

Exhaling slowly, Alexa nodded. "We had to. I had started seeing Danny when my husband and I were separated for awhile. I met him when my car had a flat tire and I was waiting for the auto club. Danny stopped and helped me and we just started talking, I guess. When Garth and I decided to give things one more try, well, of course I ended things with Danny immediately."

Danny playing the good Samaritan? Interesting. Alexa was lucky she was pretty, because if she hadn't been she might have found herself robbed instead of helped.

"How long were you seeing Danny?" Presley queried, her expression sympathetic. Seth was happy to leave this questioning to his wife.

"About three months." Alexa leaned forward, her expression earnest. "Listen, I know that Danny wasn't completely truthful with me all the time but he was fun and unpredictable. At that point in my life I needed someone who wanted to have a good time and didn't want some sort of commitment. Danny fit the bill." Alexa smiled at the memories. "He was pretty wild and he was just what I needed then. He was so full of life. We went dancing and drinking and listened to bands. It's hard to believe that he's gone."

This Danny sure sounded different than the one Brittany described or the one that Seth had seen in the courtroom.

"And when you ended the relationship, you never talked or saw him again? Not even phone calls or maybe a text?"

"No, it was a clean break. We decided it would be better that way."

Presley snuck a glance at Seth before continuing on. "When you and Danny were together, did he ever talk about a fishing cabin that he liked to visit? Perhaps you went there with him?"

Seth held his breath waiting for her reply. If she answered yes it would make his life so much easier.

"He did but I never went there. I'm not much into fishing but he went alone a few times. He loved that cabin." Alexa frowned and fidgeted in her seat. "I'm not sure how all of this is helping you. What are you trying to find out exactly?"

Disappointment crashed through him but it was quickly followed by determination. He'd find another way.

Seth cleared his throat. "When Danny was apprehended the money from the bank heist was missing. We're still looking for it and we thought you might know of somewhere he felt comfortable enough to have hid it. Or maybe someone he trusted enough to hold it for him?"

"He never mentioned anyone that he trusted. Not really, but I suppose he might have trusted Eric."

Eric? Now this was interesting.

Rubbing his jaw, Seth tried to be as delicate as possible. "Just what did Danny tell you about himself, Mrs. Lansford?"

"He was divorced and in business with his brother. They were close as his parents had died in a tragic car accident when they were young. He liked sports and his dream was to see the Super Bowl in person. Of course I knew that half of it was probably a lie but it didn't matter one way or the other. We had fun and that's all I cared about. I wasn't going to marry him or anything."

"Divorced?" Presley choked out. "And in business with Eric? Did you ever meet Danny's brother?"

"Once or twice. He seemed like a nice person."

What a tangled web Danny had weaved. One woman who hated him and one who liked him but didn't believe a word out of his mouth. Plus Eric might have been closer to his brother than they'd been led to believe.

Just what was the truth?

Presley hummed as she cooked dinner, her spirits up despite their mixed bag of answers from Danny's girlfriends today. They had even more unanswered questions now than they'd had this morning but they had learned a few new things, too.

That Danny was a little bit of a chameleon and Eric Harbaugh might have more going on than they'd thought, if anything Alexa had been told was real. Both Presley and Seth had assumed the private eye was telling the truth – and he may have been, as much as he was aware – but clearly there was another story if Alexa Lansford was correct in saying that Eric and Danny were close.

It was still strange though, that if that was the case why didn't Eric know where the money was? Had Danny told him one location and then hid it somewhere else? His cellmate said that Danny didn't trust anyone but Alexa had a different point of view. But then she thought that Danny was *fun and harmless*, so perhaps her perception of events couldn't be relied on.

But all of that wasn't the reason Presley was in a great mood. She was happy because for the first time in a long time she and Seth were really working as a team and spending time together. It felt like lately they had their own projects, their own priorities and they were off doing what needed to be done. Separately. Even the parenting chores were often divvied up between them but this case was a whole different animal. They were doing it together and it felt like the old days when they were on the run and had no one to depend on but each other. She shouldn't romanticize those days but sometimes she couldn't help it. When there's only one human being in the world you can trust, you get pretty close to them.

Seth came up behind her and wrapped his arms around her waist, kissing her temple. "Hey babe, Mom and Dad want to Skype about seven our time. Does that sound good? Then we can read Ben and Lulu their story and say goodnight before they go to bed."

The kids were having a wonderful time and George and Marion were loving showing off their grandchildren to their friends. Presley missed them terribly but this little bit of independence was good for everyone.

At least that's what she kept telling herself.

"Sounds fine. I made cheeseburgers for dinner. I hope that's okay."

Seth grinned and rubbed his stomach. "Did you put the Worcestershire sauce in the ground beef?"

He loved it when she did that. It was cute that it didn't take much to make him happy.

She nodded. "And garlic, too."

"Hot damn. Maybe I'll have two tonight."

She hoped so because she'd made three and a half burgers, and only one was for her. The half was for Fergus.

"Grab a plate and I'll dish it up."

Burgers and buns quickly rested on the plates, along with some frozen veggies she'd dug out of the freezer. There had to be at least one healthy food. They'd barely dug into their meal when Seth's phone began to vibrate.

Presley wrinkled her nose and sighed. "I guess you better answer it. It's probably Hank and he needs you to go into the office."

Seth picked up the phone and shook his head. "It's Tanner returning my call. I really do need to take this."

"Put it on speaker then so you don't have to repeat back the conversation later."

Seth tapped on the screen and Tanner's voice boomed through the kitchen. "I called because Dare has some good news."

"We could use some," Seth laughed. "Today was frustrating to say the least. Each of Danny's girlfriends described him a little differently, and Alexa Lansford also told us that Eric and Danny were close, which is just the opposite of what we'd heard before. This whole case gets murkier with every passing day so I'm glad that you have some good news for us."

"It sounds like Eric leads a far more interesting life for real than he does on paper," Tanner observed. "I talked to Evan earlier today, by the way, and they haven't found Eric yet. He was kind of getting the idea that they weren't looking all that hard. His witness protection was voluntary and if he doesn't want to be in it then they can't force him. Evan did say that they checked Eric's friends and neighbors and he hasn't returned home. He could be anywhere and he's not using his credit cards or they would know where he was located."

Presley simply wasn't sure what to believe anymore. Was Eric the innocent brother who had no idea what his brother was up to? Or had he known and maybe even been part of it? She felt pretty sure that he hadn't known where the cash was hidden because he'd sent someone after her and Seth. When she thought about it too hard her head hurt. Nothing made sense.

"So what's the good news?" Seth asked. "We could use some."

Tanner chuckled at the sound of desperation in Seth's voice. "Dare's property searches turned up something kind of interesting. It might be nothing but it could be what you've been looking for. For about a year when they were first married, Danny and Lyndsey Harbaugh lived next door to Charlotte and Jim Styles. Now here's the fun part... Charlotte and Jim Styles have a small piece of property near Glistening Lake. You know how we all feel about coincidences."

Seth didn't believe in them but he did believe in tedious police research and Dare had done an outstanding job.

"Were they friends with the Styles? Would the Styles have lent their fishing cabin to Danny?"

"Dare couldn't find out any details with just a computer search. Hell, Danny may not have even met the Styles and there may not be a fishing shack on the property. Lots of neighbors never talk to each other but it sounds like something that needs to be checked out. I'll send you the information."

Finally, a lead they could actually follow. The day wasn't a total loss after all.

# CHAPTER TWENTY-SIX

B leary-eyed but armed with strong coffee, Seth and Presley
had set off before dawn to find the hunting cabin with the
scant directions they were able to get from Tanner. Seth had
been unsure about bringing Presley but when she'd told him that
Eliza had terrible morning sickness again and that they wouldn't
be meeting at the coffee shop, he'd known right then that he
wouldn't be able to talk her out of going. She was enjoying this
detective work far too much. Besides, he'd pitched in most
nights since they returned from Vegas and almost everything but
the final touches were ready for the grand opening at the
beginning of the month.

He was certainly proud of Presley and all of her hard work.
This coffee shop was her dream. She was tough on herself about
the past but no one could now say she wasn't ambitious.

The drive, however, was uneventful and he and Presley spent
most of it making plans for upgrades to the house. With two
growing children, it was beginning to feel small and not unlike
an overstuffed toy chest. The situation was likely to get worse
before it got better, so they'd both conceded that perhaps they
needed to think about adding on maybe a family room and

another bathroom. Lulu was going to be a teenage girl someday – perish the thought – and she'd probably spend most of her
time in the bathroom if Presley was to be believed.

"I don't know that I'll ever get over all these mountains
around me," Presley marveled. "It's so flat in Florida. But
warm."

His girl did suffer the cold and she missed the beaches every
now and then, despite living in Montana for years. Who was he
kidding? Sometimes he hated the cold, too.

"But we have snow-capped mountains and beautiful lakes."

"That's true. It is beautiful out here. I can see why Danny
Harbaugh loved it so much."

Seth was trying to see this situation through Danny's eyes.
Was it the remoteness of the location that appealed to him? The
sheer beauty of the mountains? Or had it been something else
altogether?

"We're getting close. Keep your eyes peeled for a side road
or even just a path."

Presley craned her neck to get a better view. "We're already
on a side of a side road. Is this even on a map?"

Rutted and rough, the dirt road was on no map that Seth
knew of and Tanner's instructions had been vague, but after
studying a map of the property there were a few places that
stood out as better locations for a hunting cabin. This was the
first on his list. Sometimes a man just had to follow his instincts.

"There." Presley pointed to a break in the trees. "It's barely a
road, though. Do you think we can get the truck back there?"

Seth pulled the vehicle off to the side. "I'll take a look. Stay
here where it's warm."

Hopping out of the truck cab, the chillier mountain air at
this altitude hit Seth hard, making him pull his jacket closer
around his body. Luckily, though, he didn't have to walk far to

see that his truck would make it, although it would be tight. Hurrying back to the vehicle, he swung into the driver's side to deliver the news.

"We're good to go, at least as far as I could see. If we get to a point where we have to stop, I'll get out and walk."

Caution was deeply ingrained in Seth so he drove slowly up the winding road, the branches from the trees brushing against the sides of his truck. It was narrower than he'd originally thought, but it was passable and that's all that Seth could ask for. He really didn't want to have to hike this property but he would if he had to. Wherever this cabin was located it was far away from anyone else.

*That's probably what appealed to Danny. Not the hunting or the scenery. The location.*

Just when Seth thought he'd chosen the wrong spot a cabin came into view in the distance. Small and rundown, it wasn't much more than it had been described – a hunting shack. Immediately he stopped the truck and backed it up slightly, but they could still see the shack in the distance.

"What are you doing?" Presley asked, looking in front of them and then behind. "We're going the wrong way."

Seth shook his head and smiled grimly. "We're going the absolute right way. Didn't you see the smoke coming out of the chimney? There's someone in that cabin and I don't want them to see us driving up."

"Some detective I am," Presley laughed, smacking her forehead. "I didn't notice that. I was too busy looking for a car parked out front."

Seth had looked for that too but only briefly. "They could have parked behind the building or some trees. And don't be too hard on yourself. You're not a cop, remember?"

Killing the engine, Seth reached behind him to gather up his supplies. His service revolver was tucked under his coat but he was also going to take his shotgun as well. Once again caution was the order of the day. He didn't feel that the situation was necessarily dangerous. He wouldn't have brought Presley otherwise, no matter how much she complained. But this was the unknown and if he'd learned anything in the Army and then law enforcement was that he should always be prepared. Whoever was residing in that cabin might be friendly or they might not. At the very least they'd be surprised about a visitor.

"Stay here in the warmth of the truck," Seth instructed in his most no-nonsense tone. "I'm going to talk to the inhabitant of the house and ask if I can look around a little bit. If I'm lucky they may actually let me."

"If you're lucky they won't even be home and you can look around all you want without them knowing," Presley laughed. "That would be easier."

It would be but he wasn't that lucky.

"And you'll stay put?" Seth hesitated as he climbed out of the truck. "Promise me, Presley."

Rolling her eyes dramatically and sighing, she raised her right hand. "I promise. You know, the lack of trust in our marriage is disturbing. I said I would stay here."

"I trust you but I also know you. Don't leave the truck."

He could hear her snort as he shut the door and locked it behind him. People in hunting and fishing cabins tended to be the friendly and helpful sort to their fellow outdoor sportsmen, but Seth wasn't as sure they would be open to him snooping around the property. If his first impression was anything to go by the property didn't have many places to hide money unless it was actually inside the building. There was a wood pile stacked against the side of the cabin and some trees circling the clearing but that was about it, although as he neared the structure he could see a small economy car parked behind it.

Stomping up the steps, Seth paused to take a longer look at the cabin. Although weathered, the shack was obviously well-maintained. It wasn't large but it would be warm and safe on a cold Montana night. He knocked on the door and waited but a movement from behind the curtains caught his eye.

Someone was home.

He knocked again, hoping it sounded like a friendly greeting but not really knowing how a friendly knock would sound. He wanted to make friends with whomever was inside and hope they let him wander around the property.

The door finally swung open slightly and a man stood there frowning. It took a second for the face to register with Seth, but when it did it was like he'd been smacked on the side of the head.

It was Eric Harbaugh.

# CHAPTER TWENTY-SEVEN

Still shocked at who Seth had found in the cabin, he pushed Eric Harbaugh back into the building, slamming the door shut behind him.

"Hey," Eric shouted, struggling against Seth's hold on his shirt. "What in the hell are you doing? Did Frank send you?"

Seth had a pretty good idea that Frank was from the cartel.

"No," Seth said through gritted teeth. Pissed at himself, he should have realized that Eric would hide out here. The guy wasn't a seasoned criminal and didn't know how to hide to save his life. "My name is Seth Reilly. Does that ring a bell?"

Eric's eyes went wide as saucers and his skin paled to a deathly white. Going limp, he staggered back, almost falling against the small, worn couch.

"Are you here to kill me?"

Christ on a unicycle, what did this guy think Seth was? Some sort of mobster? "No, but I am going to call the US Marshal service and tell them where you are. They're looking for you. You know, I worked really hard getting them to put you into witness protection and you just ran away. I think you have some explaining to do. Actually, you have a whole lot of explaining.

Like why you think I have the money."

Eric fell back onto the cushions of the couch, his head falling into his hands. "Everything is so fucked up and I don't know what to do."

Shit. This was not what Seth had expected when he'd knocked on the door. He needed to call Evan. He needed to get Presley out of the truck once he made sure that Eric wasn't armed because he sure didn't look dangerous. Then he needed to get some answers because there were too many questions. But first things first.

"Eric, look at me," Seth commanded, waiting for the man to comply. He finally did but his cheeks and eyes were red. "Do you have any sort of firearm here?"

He didn't answer for a minute but then he nodded, pointing to the backpack sitting on the tiny kitchen counter. It wasn't much of a kitchen actually, just a small stove and a sink with enough countertop that perhaps one person could sit there and eat.

Wasting no time, Seth retrieved a small handgun from the backpack and after emptying it, tucked it back in. Eric was now unarmed. Check.

"Stay right here for a minute and don't fucking move."

Stepping out onto the porch he waved his arms toward where the truck was parked, not sure if Presley would even be able to see him. But eventually she appeared from out behind the scrub of trees, jogging toward the house.

Presley out of the truck. Check.

Now time to talk to Eric.

Seth leaned against the counter and inspected the man who might have the answers he was looking for. Eric resembled his brother superficially. The same eyes and jaw but not as thick as Danny and not as tall either. Today, Eric looked a little worse for wear, his jaw covered in scruff and his clothes rumpled, but he appeared to be capable of discussing what was going on here, although Seth had noticed a bottle of whiskey on the floor next to the couch. Luckily it was almost full.

He decided to start with an easy question and work his way up. "How long have you been here?"

Eric took a deep breath and tried to sit straighter, although his lips still trembled. "About three days. It took me awhile to get here."

"The car out back…is it yours?"

A flush crawled up Eric's neck. "I–I stole it. I'm so sorry and of course I want to give it back but I had to have transportation and I couldn't drive my own car."

The guy was willing to commit a crime to get away from the Marshals. Interesting.

The door burst open and Presley quickly shut it behind her, shucking off her jacket.

"Hi, I'm Presley Reilly." She walked over to the fireplace and looked around the little cabin. "This is so cute."

"Honey, I'd like you to meet Eric Harbaugh. Eric, this is my wife Presley. The woman your investigator tried to kidnap."

Presley's gasp was almost drowned out by Eric's groan.

"I never wanted either of you hurt. I'm not a violent person. I just needed the money and I thought you had it. My life is on the line here."

"Maybe you better start your story at the beginning," Seth suggested. "And we'll fill in any details we know as you go. How does that sound?"

He'd made it sound like a choice but it wasn't really. Eric was going to talk whether he liked it or not.

✧ ✧ ✧ ✧

Presley perched in a scarred rocking chair near the fireplace, gobsmacked at finding Eric Harbaugh at the cabin. She hadn't expected him there, to be honest. If she were on the run, and thank goodness she wasn't anymore, she wouldn't go anywhere that was known to be a hangout of a close relative or friend. She would hide out in a completely new place that no one would expect her to be.

But then she was more experienced with death threats than Eric was. Too experienced.

Seth had taken to pacing the small little cabin, back and forth in front of the fireplace while Eric sniffled and visibly shook with fear. He should never have run from witness protection. What had he been thinking? She opened her mouth to ask but then quickly snapped it shut. As much as she wanted to ask, she couldn't derail whatever questioning Seth had planned. He'd eventually ask anyway.

Stopping in front of Eric, Seth asked his first question. "Let's start at the beginning. When did you learn that your brother Danny was out of jail?"

Eric shifted uncomfortably on the couch. "Danny called me out of the blue. I hadn't heard from him since I visited him Christmas before last. He said he was out and was going to come by and see me but he had something to take care of first that might take a few days. He said it was business with Seth Reilly that couldn't wait. But I never saw or heard from him again."

So Danny had been trying to even the score with Seth. Presley had been in danger, although Danny must have been on the run as well, owing money to dangerous people. If he still had the money, why hadn't he grabbed it quickly and paid them off before worrying about Seth? The only answer was that he *wasn't* worried. As long as he was working for the cartel he must have thought he was safe. It was only when he was dead that the cartel had become anxious for their cash.

"And how did you find out he was dead?"

"Some guy named Frank showed up at my office telling me that I owed them twenty thousand because Danny had lost a shipment and couldn't pay it back. They said he was dead. I wasn't all that shocked. Danny always lived on the edge."

"Did Danny say anything about the bank robbery money?" Seth asked. "Or about owing the cartel?"

"No." Eric shook his head, his voice choked with tears. "He just said he was going to come see me, that's it. Then that scary guy Frank came and said I owed all of that money. I don't have that kind of cash but I knew Danny had robbed that bank and the money was never found. I thought that if I could find it I could pay those guys back and they'd leave me alone. That's why I hired that private investigator. He said that you were the cop that arrested Danny and that you had the opportunity to take it."

A muscle ticked in Seth's jaw. "But I didn't. I was investigated and found clean."

Eric shrugged. "That's what the private eye said but he also said that cops cover for other cops, which made sense to me. We decided that he would follow you and grab your wife. Once you told him where the money was he'd let her go." He looked up at Presley, panic in his expression. "I told him not to hurt you and to treat you well. I'm not that kind of guy. Truly. I was just desperate and scared. If I didn't pay them they were going to kill me and the way Frank described my death it wasn't going to be pleasant. He said something about long and painful. I still don't even know why they came to me for the money. I mean, Danny and I have never been all that close."

Which was the opposite of what Alexa had said. More questions but they were slowly getting answers.

"I don't have the money," Seth repeated, annoyance in his

tone. "It wouldn't have mattered if I did though. Do you honestly believe that your hired private eye would have turned his back on two hundred thousand? If I did have the money and had told him the location, what do you think are the chances that he was going to run back and tell you? Let me answer that. Zero."

Eric's shoulders slumped. "We signed a contract."

Even Presley was surprised at the man's naïveté, especially when his brother was a criminal, although hardly a genius mastermind. Talk about opposites…

Seth smiled. "And let's say that you found that money and paid it to Frank? What do you think they were going to do once you did? Pat you on the head and let you walk away? That wasn't going to happen either. You were a dead man either way. The safest place for you is in witness protection. Why in the hell did you run?"

Eric hopped up from the couch, clearly agitated and fearful. "I saw Frank…or at least I thought I did. Now I'm not so sure. Everything is so messed up and I don't know what's real anymore. I think I might be going crazy. I freaked out and ran. I came here thinking I was safe, but if you found me they probably can too. Jesus, I'm a dead man."

She shouldn't interrupt but…well…staying quiet wasn't her strong suit.

"We weren't looking for you, Eric," Presley said softly, hoping it would reassure the terrified man. "We found you by accident."

That seemed to shock the man because he scratched at his head, a scowl on his face. "Then why are you here?"

"We're investigating where your brother might have hidden the money," Seth replied smoothly before Presley had a chance to. "Everyone we talked to mentioned this cabin as Danny's favorite place. The problem is that there's no way he could have put the money here himself. I captured him too far from here.

Someone had to have helped him."

Eric looked around the sparse room. "You think it's here?"

"Not necessarily," Seth said, also letting his gaze roam around the room. "But it was the only clue we had. There could be a clue here, though."

"If we could find that money, that would save my life," Eric declared, looking almost hopeful now. "Do you think you know where it is?"

"This was literally the only clue we had," Presley repeated. "We were hoping to find either the money or something else that would keep us on the trail. Instead we found you."

"And even if we did find the money," Seth warned. "We'd have to give it back to the authorities. You wouldn't get to keep it."

Eric exhaled noisily and let his head fall back on the worn cushion. "Then I'm still a walking dead man. Now what am I going to do?"

Seth held up his phone. "I'm going to call Evan and he's going to get the Marshals out here to get you. You're going back into protection, and don't fucking run away again. They can keep you safe. And if you see someone that you think is with the cartel, tell the agent assigned to you. Do not take this into your own hands. Do you understand?"

Eric fell back onto the sofa. "I'm just an IT consultant. I don't know anything about this cloak and dagger stuff."

He looked so defeated and Presley felt sorry for him. "You've done a pretty good job. You're still alive. Not everyone would be."

"That's true but for how long?"

On his own, the odds weren't in his favor but with help? He just might survive.

# CHAPTER TWENTY-EIGHT

Presley and Seth had loaded Eric into the truck and headed back to Harper where they were supposed to meet a couple of US Marshals. They would pick up Eric and take him off to hide somewhere until the DEA, at some point in the near or far future, decided to bring down the cartel. Eric was rather morose about leaving his life behind and starting a new one and Presley was trying to cheer him up. He looked like he'd lost his best friend which he had, in a way. He wasn't going to see his friends again and she was the only other person in that vehicle who understood how that felt.

"I won't know anyone," Eric lamented as they sped down the highway. "I'll be completely alone."

She remembered what Alexa had said about Eric and Danny. "Were you close to your family?"

"Not really," Eric replied. "Danny was always different than me when we were growing up. Always in trouble, always pushing boundaries. Our parents died when we were young so you'd think that would bring us closer, but it really didn't. We went to live with an aunt but Danny just became even more out of control. He left home the minute he turned eighteen. I stayed on through college but Aunt Lena eventually died. She'd mortgaged the place to the hilt for my education and then Danny was in and out of prison, of course."

Presley snuck a glance at her husband but he was wearing a bland expression and keeping his gaze trained on the road ahead of them.

"One of Danny's girlfriends said you and your brother were close. That you spent a lot of time together and that he was a partner in your consulting business."

Why not find out what Eric would say about Alexa's story? They were all stuck together in the truck for the duration of the trip.

Laughing, Eric shook his head. "That must have been...what was her name? Anna? Danny asked me to do that. Said he was turning over a new leaf and divorcing Lyndsey. I wanted to believe him but it didn't last long. He was going to go straight and wanted me to pretend that he was an upstanding, boring guy. That's how he described it too. I guess that's what I am. Upstanding and boring."

"You stole a car." Seth's voice was amused and hard at the same time. "That's hardly upstanding. Or boring."

Eric grinned and slapped his knee. "I'll be damned, I guess for the first time in my life I'm interesting. And I have Danny to thank. They can put that on my tombstone."

"There aren't going to be any tombstones," Presley protested. "Let's think positive."

"You're right," Eric agreed. "I'm positive I'm going to be the victim of a grisly murder. How's that?"

"You're a tough guy to cheer up," Seth observed, although he never took his eyes off the road. "Kind of glass half full kind of person, huh?"

Seth wasn't helping but Presley had the feeling he wasn't

trying. Her husband was annoyed that all they'd found at the cabin was Eric Harbaugh and now finding the money looked impossible. They had no other leads.

"I have to leave my entire life because a drug cartel wants me dead. I don't think anything positive is going to come out of that. Sorry, I guess I'm a little depressed."

"You'll make new friends," Presley said in what she hoped was a soothing tone. "Better friends. Just think about this way…you get a chance at a brand new life. Not many people have that opportunity. You can become anybody you want to."

Eric gave her a crooked smile. "James Bond is taken, but I guess you have a point. My old life wasn't all that fantastic. My business was doing okay but nothing to shout about. Most of my buddies are either married with kids and don't have time to hang out or they're like me, divorced with no money. The few that do have money are dating twentysomethings. My family's all gone and the only thing I have left are the memories. They can't take those from me."

"You see, it might be a good thing. You could end up with a really terrific life. At least you'll be alive. That's a positive thing."

Presley's gift at getting people to talk about themselves was working in high gear today because Eric couldn't seem to stop talking.

"Breathing is good," Eric agreed. "I'm so pissed at my brother right now, though. He's caused me trouble my whole life and now this. I know he didn't intend to die in that explosion but he's certainly left me holding the bag. But of course, that's nothing new either. I was always bailing him out of trouble when we were kids. I thought Aunt Lena was going to rip her hair out a few times, God rest her soul. I remember all the times that Danny would hide in the space under the barn until Aunt Lena had calmed down a little. Later when he was older, he'd just take off for a few days. Eventually Danny just moved out. She said he was turning into a hoodlum. I guess she was right."

From the signs on the road, they were getting close to Harper and soon Eric would be turned over to the US Marshals. Presley sent up a wish that his new life would be as good as hers had turned to be. It sounded like he deserved a break.

"I'm sorry about your aunt," Presley said. "All my family is gone too."

She didn't count Nora, her stepsister, as family anymore. Once a relative takes out a hit on your life and tries to frame you for arms dealing they get cut out of the family tree. If events had gone another way Presley could easily be serving a life sentence in federal prison.

"I miss her and I was sad to sell the home and property, but it was mortgaged to the hilt so I had no choice. Now it's part of the Perry ranch. They're buying up everything around these parts. Soon they'll own everything between here and Springwood."

Presley hadn't missed the sound of Seth's quietly indrawn breath. His knuckles gripping the steering wheel were white.

"Did you say that your former family home is now part of the Perry ranch? Whereabouts?"

"On the west side of the Perry place. Closer to Springwood than Harper. Near the lake."

Near the lake. Now Presley understood what Seth was getting at.

Because that was damn close to where Seth had found and arrested Danny Harbaugh.

Could the money be there?

✧ ✧ ✧ ✧

After a quick call to the agents coming to pick up Eric, Seth pointed the truck toward the Perry ranch, the home of Angus Perry, one of the largest landowners in the area. Seth knew from experience that if anyone was sniffing around the ranch, Perry would know about it. He was constantly bombarding the sheriff's station with calls regarding would-be cattle rustlers. The rancher took paranoia to a whole new level.

Pulling in front of the large house, Seth could only hope that Angus was at home. Despite his failing health, he liked to be out on the land and overseeing the day to day workings. His two sons had taken over a couple of years ago, but Angus still had a firm hand on the reins.

"Just stay here in the truck while I talk to Angus real quick. It won't take long."

Eric nodded his agreement but Presley gave him a dirty look. He would have taken her in with him but someone needed to watch Eric. He pulled his service revolver and handed it to his wife.

"Shoot him if he tries to make a run for it."

Eric looked startled but Presley finally smiled. She now understood why she was staying in the truck.

"Will do."

"I taught her everything I know about marksmanship," Seth told a wide-eyed Eric. "So if I were you, I'd stay put."

His sweet and pretty wife was a damn good shot. He'd made sure of that after the first time she'd had killers after her.

Swinging out of the truck, he bounded up the front porch steps and rang the doorbell. He only had to wait a moment and then the door opened. Angus. That was good. This really shouldn't take long then.

"Angus, got a minute to talk?"

The older man nodded and stepped back to let Seth pass into the small foyer.

OLIVIA JAYMES

"What can I help you with, Sheriff? Is it rustlers again?"

Seth wished that was all it was. This was much more complicated.

"I wanted to ask if you'd seen anyone recently looking around that parcel of land you purchased from Lena Harbaugh's estate. Man or woman? It's important, Angus."

The older man scowled and shook his head. "I haven't seen anyone. We use it for storage mostly. I haven't even bothered to knock down the house yet. Why? What's so important about that parcel of land?"

Probably nothing. But maybe something.

"Not a lot but I'd like to see. Do you mind if I take a look around? I don't have a warrant so I'll need your permission."

Angus shrugged. "Sure, you can look around. It's just a plot of land, though."

It might just be the answer to the question Seth had been asking himself for years. It might be the location of the bank money.

Striding down the front steps and back to the truck, Seth pulled out his cell phone and dialed Tanner, who would be closest to the location. He'd have jurisdiction.

"Tanner? It's Seth. I think I might be on to something. There's a possibility that Danny Harbaugh hid the money on a piece of property that used to be owned by his aunt but is now part of the Perry ranch. It's near the lake. I'll send you the directions. Presley and I could use a hand searching it. I don't suppose...?"

The chuckle on the other end of the phone had Seth smiling. Help was on the way.

"Let me gather a few more people and we'll be on our way. I hope this is it."

"No problem. I have to stop off at the sheriff's station and

218

hand over Eric Harbaugh to a couple of US Marshals."

"What? Wait...when did...? You have Harbaugh? Damn, I think there's a bunch of this story that I missed."

That was an understatement.

"Just meet me at the location in about an hour and I'll tell you everything. But I'm not sure you're going to believe it."

The mystery that had bothered Seth for years just might be solved today.

# CHAPTER TWENTY-NINE

E ric had been reluctantly returned to the US Marshals. Two extremely nice agents had met them at the sheriff's station and had taken him into protective custody. Presley had tried one last time to convey to him that he was being given a huge chance to start his life all over again and she might have succeeded. By the time he was loaded into a dark-windowed SUV he was almost smiling, although quite nervous. She didn't blame him. Starting all over again was a daunting task but she had a feeling he was going to be fine.

And he'd promised not to run away again.

She'd only known him for a few hours, but in reality she'd felt like she'd known him for years. She couldn't tell him that, though. Even now, she and Seth kept her origin story quiet. Not because they were afraid but because it brought up so many questions that frankly she didn't want to talk about. The past was the past and best left there.

Seth pulled up to the small parcel of land and parked the truck. "Let's walk the area and see if we can find anything, but let's stick together."

"Because looking for bank robbery money is romantic?"

"Because I don't want you getting lost and then having to find you, too."

Sticking out her tongue, she brushed past him to walk around the perimeter of the old house. "Other husbands would have just agreed with me."

"Other husbands wouldn't even have you here. Your cute little bottom would be sitting at home."

At least he'd called it cute. Romantic man. He might get laid tonight.

"I wonder what other couples do when they spend quality time together?" Presley wondered out loud, giggling at the scowl on her husband's face. He hadn't been as amused by Eric as she had. "On our tenth anniversary will you take me out on a search for a dead body?"

"Oh, for fuck's sake," he growled. "I thought you wanted to be here."

"I do," she assured him with a laugh. "But come on, Seth. Even you have to admit this is funny. Other couples don't spend their free time the way we do. It's not a complaint – I love it. It's just an observation."

At first she'd thought he was going to growl at her again but then his smile widened, turning into a grin. Laughing, he pulled her into a hug and dropped a chaste kiss on her lips.

"I never thought about it that way before. I guess we're not exactly Ozzie and Harriet."

"What do you know about Ozzie and Harriet?" Presley laughed. "Have you ever even seen them on television? I know I haven't."

Chuckling, Seth led the way to the barn. They'd found nothing around the house. "I haven't either but I remember my parents talking about them. Apparently, they had the perfect American family. Or maybe that was the Cleavers, Ward and

June? That show I did see but in reruns."

She'd seen *Leave it to Beaver* and the image of Seth as Eddie Haskell had her giggling, her hand over her mouth to try and cover it up but Seth was on to her.

"What's so funny? Your face is all red."

"*You look so lovely today, Mrs. Cleaver,*" Presley mimicked. "I was just picturing you as Eddie."

That got a smile out of Seth. "I was more like the Beaver. But we had a friend a little like Eddie. Always kissing up to adults."

She'd never heard this story from Seth and she'd thought she'd heard everything. Multiple times.

"What happened to him?"

"Dale is the mayor. Now he kisses up to everyone…for votes."

Sometimes Seth's deadpan delivery was simply a riot. He had her leaning against the old barn, holding her stomach as she pictured Seth with a little Dale Fincham, debating on stage. People were always trying to get Seth to run against Fincham and Seth always said no. She now had a better idea as to why. He didn't like kissing up to anyone.

"You've never told me this before."

"You never asked."

She sighed in annoyance. "And yet you tell the same stories over and over so many times I'm beginning to think they're my memories, not yours."

"Are you saying I need to get some new material?"

"I'm just saying that you probably have other stories. I wouldn't mind hearing them."

Presley stopped and studied the area around the barn. Trees and an old tractor. Not much else. This was turning out to be a complete waste of time. "I don't think about the past all that much, to be honest."

That was true. Instead he was always thinking about the future, planning carefully and studying his options.

"I'll just ask your mom. She loves to talk about when you were a kid."

"You can ask but she gets all of us mixed up. You're just as likely to hear a story about Sam or Jason as you are me. None of us were angels, although Sam will try and say he was. Don't believe it."

"Are you saying that Sam is not a credible witness to his own past?"

Seth snorted and checked behind an old shed. "No, I'm saying he's full of shit."

"Can I ask you another question?"

"Can I stop you?"

Blowing out an impatient breath, she gave her husband a mean look. "Funny. Seriously though, what are we looking for? Is it one of those where we'll know it when we see it? Because I haven't seen anything even remotely interesting. It can't be anywhere obvious or Perry and his men would have found it."

"But he can't have dug a deep hole to bury it because he didn't have time," Seth said. "Or traveled too far from the main area here. I think at most he had a ten-minute lead on me. I also doubt he would have tried to go into the house. Eric said that Danny and the aunt didn't see eye to eye. He might have thought she'd turn him in."

Presley's gaze ran over the tractor, barn, and a scrub of bushes and trees. "That doesn't leave us with much. I do think he'd want to hide it well enough that the elements or wildlife wouldn't get to it, though. So I don't think he would have shoved it in a tree."

"Good point," Seth agreed, his own gaze traversing the

property. "He'd want to keep it safe and dry, plus hidden well enough that no one was going to accidentally stumble onto it."

Harbaugh would want to keep it hidden well, especially from his aunt who was still living here at the time. And where better to hide the money than where Danny had hidden successfully all those times he'd been in trouble?

"Seth, I think I know where he hid the money." Excitedly, she grabbed his arm and tugged him toward the barn. "Remember when Eric said that Danny hid in some room under the barn when he was in trouble with his aunt? Wouldn't that be the first place he'd go to hide the money?"

She could tell from Seth's puzzled expression that he hadn't been listening to Eric's stories all that closely, instead concentrating on driving. But dammit, he should have been. This was important.

"Aren't you glad that people want to tell me their life story? Because Eric said that Danny hid out in some sort of room under the barn," she explained again. "Maybe like a cellar? If we find it, I bet we find the money."

Seth rubbed his chin. "I am glad, and honey, you're a genius."

"Naturally," she sighed, acting quite put upon. "If only you'd admit it more."

"But if I picked you for a wife, doesn't that make me a genius too? In fact, maybe even more so."

They stepped into the barn and left the doors open so the sun would shine in to the dim interior.

"It makes you lucky, not a genius. Now let's look for this room."

Like most old barns everything was covered in dirt and dust. Presley's skin crawled and within seconds she wanted a shower. It was hot and grimy and kind of spooky. Clearly she'd seen way too many horror movies in her lifetime.

Moving a wheelbarrow aside, Seth uncovered a door in the floor. "This must be it. It was probably used as a root cellar when the barn was built as I'm guessing this hole in the ground is older than the house."

"It's not even hidden all that well," Presley observed. "Aunt Lena never looked for Danny here?"

"Maybe she didn't want to find him," Seth said, grunting with the effort to lift the heavy door. Years of dirt flew into the air, making them both choke and cough. "Maybe she was content to let him hide while she cooled off."

She peered down into the darkness. "I don't suppose there's a light switch?"

Chuckling, Seth shook his head and stood. "I've got a flashlight right here in my pocket."

He pulled out his cell phone and hit a few buttons.

"That's not a flashlight. That's a flashlight app."

"I've got a flashlight in the truck but I don't want to go back. This will do. Looks like there's a ladder to climb down." Seth shined the light into the cellar. "It's not even that deep or large. You stay here and I'll go down and check."

Presley wasn't sure she liked the look of that old wooden ladder. Would it even hold Seth's weight? Presumably the last time anybody had used it was years ago.

"Maybe I should go." Presley clutched at Seth's arm. "I'm lighter than you are and that ladder doesn't look too sturdy."

"It's from when things were made to last. It will be fine."

*Fine. It will be fine.*

That's what Seth always said and most of the time he was right. But wasn't he due to be wrong?

"Why don't you wait for Tanner and the others to get here?"

"Honey," Seth said gently, bringing her grimy fingers up to

his lips. "I'll be okay. The cellar looks really small and shallow. Even if the ladder broke I think I could climb out of there without too much trouble."

There was no sense arguing, not when he was like this. Stubborn. Hard-headed. The last time she'd tried they hadn't spoken to each other for hours, each one pretending that the other wasn't in the house. She didn't want a repeat performance.

"Fine," she huffed. "But be careful. If you get hurt, you'll have to wait for Tanner to drag you out of there because I can't lift you."

With the phone in his right hand, Seth quickly descended the ladder into the cellar. He was right that the room wasn't that big. Once he was down there, she was able to see that the space wasn't much more than five by five with low ceilings. Seth was stooped over so he wouldn't hit his head. He could definitely climb out without any trouble.

"There are some shelves on the wall," he called up, his voice muffled slightly. "I think I found something. Step back."

Heart racing with excitement, Presley waited as two black bags emblazoned with the bank name on one side in gold lettering flew up and landed at her feet.

"My God, we found it," Presley said. She was staring right at the bank bags but it was almost too much to comprehend. This money had been missing for years but now here it was. "I can't believe we found it."

The sound of footsteps behind Presley had her whirling around.

"I was hoping you would. Now step away from the money."

Brittany. Holding a gun pointed right at Presley.

This was the third time her life was in danger. This was becoming a really bad habit.

# CHAPTER THIRTY

Seth had stared down the barrel of a gun a few times in his life and come out the other side to talk about it, but this time it wasn't him. That gun was pointed directly at Seth's heart.

In other words, right at Presley.

He could feel his blood running cold in his veins and his heart galloping in his chest, loud enough for the whole county to hear. Adrenaline had kicked in hard, that fight or flight instinct that he had to wrestle for control.

Because his caveman instincts could get his wife killed. This wasn't the moment to go off half-cocked without a thought. No, he needed to keep calm. Cool.

In control. Only then would he be able to get both of them out of this alive.

Presley, of course, would laugh at his thoughts. He knew what she thought of his penchant for control in every situation but for once he truly needed it.

He could – and would – fall apart later. Once Presley was safe.

"Brittany." He was shocked by how smooth his voice sounded. "I'm surprised to see you here."

He took a slow, calculated step up one rung on the ladder.

The woman took a step forward but the gun never wavered from Presley's chest. Although about eight feet away, she could make the shot from there and probably not miss. This was Montana and knowing the way around a firearm wasn't unusual, but few people had actually shot another human being. That was a whole different thing than shooting at a target or maybe a nuisance animal. Did Brittany have what it took to shoot a woman – a mother – in cold blood? Seth wasn't going to take the chance and find out.

"Go ahead and stay down in the cellar, Sheriff. No need for you to move."

Holding his hands up in a non-threatening manner, Seth did as he was told but all the while his mind was working...looking...searching...for just a smidgen of an opportunity to distract Brittany. He only needed a split second and he could completely change the advantage from her to him. She wasn't a powerful woman; to the contrary, she was smaller than Presley, who barely skimmed his shoulder. The only thing Brittany Smithers had going for her was a gun and the element of surprise. One of those was gone now.

A quick glance at his wife told him that Presley was holding up well being on the wrong end of a gun barrel. A sheen of sweat covered her face and her lips trembled slightly, but someone who didn't know her like he did wouldn't see the fear. She was afraid but his brave woman wasn't about to show it. She'd learned a lot since the day he'd met her straight off that plane from Florida. That night she'd been freezing cold, tired, terrified, and the most beautiful woman he'd ever seen in his life. He was pretty sure his fate had been sealed right there and then.

Now all he had to do was save her life. One more time. Then he was going to keep her locked in the house so she couldn't get into any more trouble.

Presley also had her hands held away from her body but her gaze was darting back and forth between Brittany and Seth. Wondering and waiting for him to do something? Hopefully she wouldn't have to wait long.

When Brittany glanced at Presley, he stepped up another rung. He just needed two more.

"No need to point that at us," Seth said in his most soothing tone, as if he was talking to Ben or Lulu when they scraped their knee or got a shot at the doctor. "We're all friends here."

But thoughts of his children didn't help him think more clearly and he had to ruthlessly push them out of his mind and give laser-like focus to the woman in front of him. He wanted to watch her every move, eye twitch, and breath. At some point not too far in the future he was going to have to anticipate what she was going to do.

"We're not friends, but I do appreciate all the work you've done finding Danny's money. It's going to solve all of my problems."

"You didn't know where it was?" Presley asked and Seth's chest tightened in terror. He didn't want her antagonizing Brittany. They all needed to keep the emotional level low.

Brittany smiled and shook her head. "Not at all, but I figured out after you two came to talk to me that you were looking for it. I figured that if I followed you I would find out where it was and it worked. Danny was a lousy boyfriend but this helps make up for it."

He didn't remind her that she had chosen Danny, so she had the bad taste in men. Money probably wasn't going to fix that.

If he couldn't reason with her perhaps he could scare her. "Brittany, let's talk about this. There's a group of lawmen on the way here and you don't want to go to jail. Trust me when I say it's a bad place."

"You arrived alone. I know because I followed you. You dropped off that guy and drove here. Now I'm going to take that money and get my life back on track. After I got laid off, I lost my house and my dignity. The car I drive is a piece of shit and I wait tables in a crappy diner. This money will fix all of that and Danny owes it to me. I can take it and start a new life somewhere else. Maybe somewhere warm and sunny, away from everyone who feels sorry for me. Look at Brittany, she messed up her life so don't be like her."

The woman was beginning to get agitated and that made Seth nervous. He could feel the sweat pooling at the back of his neck and trickling down his back where his shirt stuck to the skin. His heart was pounding so loudly it was like a freight train in his ears.

But he didn't move. Not a flinch. Not even a deep breath. Show no fear.

"You aren't a criminal," Presley said softly. "Not really. You'll have to live with yourself."

Brittany's chin wobbled and her eyes were bright with tears. "I've followed all the rules. Done everything I was supposed to do. Work hard. Go to school and get a good education. Work harder. Be a good person. And where did it get me? Flat broke with nothing. Maybe Danny had the right idea. Take what you want and screw everyone else."

Her arm wavered and Seth had to grit his teeth together to control his impulse to jump out of the cellar and tackle Brittany. That had death for all of them written all over it. At first his plan had been to delay until Tanner arrived but from the woman's emotional state that didn't look like it was going to be possible. He'd have to go to Plan B.

Just as soon as he thought of it.

"But look what happened to him," Seth pointed out. "Prison and then a violent death. You don't want that. Put the gun down and let's talk about this. You don't want to hurt anyone. You're not that kind of person."

Although she clearly had some moral compass issues if she was planning on gunning them down and taking the money. He didn't say that aloud however, his attention split between Brittany and Presley. His wife was holding firm but he could see her beginning to waver, the tension taking its toll. While he was fine with drawing this out for a long time, she couldn't take much more. Her body was beginning to wilt, her shoulders slumping with fatigue. He already knew what thoughts were running through her mind. The same ones were running through his as well.

Ben. Lulu. His parents and siblings. Their friends. Hell, even old Fergus. Their home. And most of all their future that they'd spent so much time planning and working for. He wasn't about to let Brittany Smithers take that away from them. Not while he still had breath in his lungs.

Brittany's fingers tightened on the gun. "I'm tired of losing. This money can change everything for me."

"Then take it," Seth urged, his throat scratchy from dust and fear. "We won't stop you. Just take it and drive away. We'll just pretend we never found it."

But Brittany was already shaking her head. "You're a cop. I can't trust you. I can't leave any witnesses."

A few tears had slipped down Presley's sweat-covered cheeks and her hands were shaking. A powerful force rose up inside of Seth to protect his woman and keep her safe from harm. He might not come out of this alive but she was going to.

"You're going to just shoot us?" Presley asked, her voice choked. "In cold blood? We have two babies."

Brittany was also covered in sweat now and the only color in her face was her brown eyes. Her lips were pressed so tightly together they had disappeared completely and the hand that held the gun was shaking. She didn't want to do this but she'd backed herself into a corner. And there was nothing more dangerous than an animal that was cornered. He needed to make her feel like she had options.

"I can't let you live. You'll tell."

Seth stepped up one more rung on the ladder. He was high enough that he could place his hands on the dirt floor or even reach out and touch the money bags.

Presley wasn't going to hold out much longer and Brittany looked like she might shoot them or faint. He wasn't sure which. Something had to be done right now. No more waiting, no more stalling. All he needed was to distract Brittany for a moment. But how? She wasn't a seasoned criminal and her nerves looked like they were stretched to the point of breaking. Perhaps he could take advantage of that.

"You haven't even checked inside the bags," Seth said, his heart banging against his ribs. He only had one shot at this so it had to work. "What if the money is gone?"

Frowning, Brittany's eyes widened. "Didn't you already look?"

Shrugging, Seth acted as innocent as possible. "I didn't have time and it was too dark down there."

"Shit," Brittany cursed and did exactly what he'd hoped she'd do. She began to rush forward but then seemed to think better of it, but it was too late. She was only a few feet away. Close enough.

His trembling fingers dug into the soft earth of the barn floor, grabbing two handfuls of dirt and small rocks. Just when she came to a skidding halt, he threw up his hands, the soil flying into Brittany's eyes and blinding her momentarily.

Just long enough.

Awash with unleashed energy, he lunged from his position on the ladder, sweeping her legs out from under her so that she dropped the gun. It skidded off to the side and Presley, thinking quickly, scampered after it. He'd tell her later how proud of her he was. She'd been strong and brave but that was the woman he loved. She was the glue that held their family together.

Brittany was not only much smaller than him; she was also not in the best of shape, either. He quickly had her subdued, although she hadn't stopped screaming and clawing at him, despite the hopelessness of her situation. Presley now had the gun trained on Brittany.

Blowing out a breath, he allowed himself a moment of triumph. They were going to live to see another day.

"You did good," Presley said breathlessly, but she was smiling at him as if she'd always known he'd save her. As if she'd never had any doubt. "But you took quite a chance."

"Had to. The situation was going downhill on a sled."

More expletives from Brittany but that's when Tanner decided to walk into the barn, Dare on his heels.

"Are we interrupting anything?" he asked with a smirk while Dare carefully reached for Brittany's gun, holding it between his thumb and finger after Presley handed it over.

"Just get over here and cuff her," Seth growled. "You'll probably want to arrest her, too."

Dare dragged Brittany to her feet and when she tried to scratch him, she was on the receiving end of a fierce growl that had her shutting her mouth and staying still. No one did grouchy like Dare. He slapped the cuffs on her and marched her outside leaving Tanner, Seth, Presley and the two money bags.

Tanner nudged one of the bags with his foot. "Looks like you found it. What's her part in the story? And where's Eric Harbaugh?"

Ignoring his best friend, Seth swept his wife up into his arms now that he didn't have to deal with a pissed off woman who wasn't going to get to keep two hundred thousand. Holding her tightly, he pressed his lips to hers, both of them sweaty and dirty, but he didn't care. For a while there he wasn't sure how he was going to get them out alive. But here she was in his arms and he could feel her soft skin under his palms and the beat of her heart again his, accelerating again but this time for a different reason. This time it was because he was so fucking relieved he almost couldn't breathe.

If he'd lost her…

"Don't," she said, whispering in his ear. "Trust me on this. I've learned over the years not to think of what might have happened. Just concentrate on the fact that we're both okay."

If this was what she dealt with every goddamn day when he left for work, he was going to have to quit and find some boring as fuck job where he'd be safe every fucking day. Because this had been intolerable and the thought that he was putting her through hell every time he left the house… He couldn't do it and he couldn't do it to his kids, either. They were young now, but soon they'd realize that Daddy had a dangerous job.

"I love you," he choked out, that delayed panic finally hitting him as tears burned the back of his eyes and his legs turned to jelly. "Jesus, I love you so much."

Her hands smoothed over his jaw and her eyes looked at him with such adoration it made him want to fall to his knees in gratitude. He didn't know what he'd done to deserve a woman and a life like this but he'd be grateful every damn day he was given.

"I love you too. You're my hero."

Seth would never ask for more than that.

# CHAPTER THIRTY-ONE

*A month later...*

P resley handed the vanilla latte to her customer and then a bag with a lemon cookie in it. They were Gloria's favorite of all the flavors that the coffee shop sold and they'd just come out of the oven.

Gloria gave Presley a delighted smile. "You shouldn't spoil your customers this way. We'll get used to it and demand it all the time. Please let me pay for it."

"It's my treat today," Presley laughed, tucking a napkin into the small bag that held the cookie. "I love my customers, but this is really just a ruse to make sure you keep coming back. Now how's Molly?"

Molly was Gloria's three-year-old Yorkie. Spoiled rotten and absolutely adorable. She'd recently had her teeth cleaned and was being quite the diva about it.

"Doing better," the woman sighed. "The doctor said that her gums shouldn't hurt her so much but she refuses to eat the crunchy food. But last night I made her some chicken and she ate that right up."

Fergus would have, too.

"I'm sure she'll be right as rain in a few days. But keep that cookie for yourself."

Gloria giggled and waved the small bag. "I certainly will. Thank you."

Eliza was also behind the counter loading those freshly baked cookies into the display case. Her morning sickness was beginning to wane and now she had a little baby bump.

"You made Gloria's day. These cookies are delicious." Eliza bit into one and rolled her eyes. "I'm a baking genius."

Presley wiped her hands and allowed herself to take a deep breath. The last of the morning rush was over and they'd have a little peace and quiet before the lunch crowd came in.

"You are a baking genius. You have also been here since four-thirty. Why don't you sit down and rest a little?"

With a sigh of contentment, Eliza lowered herself into a chair, stretching her legs out in front of her. "I think I will. It just sucks that I can't have a nice cappuccino to go with my break. I guess I'll have to stick to hot chocolate."

"You relax. I'm going to go in the storeroom and bring out some more paper cups. We're getting low under the counter."

Presley was ass-deep in cardboard boxes when Seth strolled in looking too damn sexy in his uniform while she was a mess. Good thing he was in love with her.

Luckily, he hadn't been called upon in the last month to save her ass again. They were both hoping to make the time in the barn the *last* time. Living a boring life didn't sound as horrible to Presley as it once had.

The whole Harbaugh case had been twisted and strange. They would probably never know why Danny hadn't gone and retrieved the money first thing when he'd been released from prison. Perhaps he hadn't been worried about the cartel and had known the money was safe for later. Safer than it would be if he had it.

Perhaps he'd been more focused on scaring Seth. After questioning the florist, they knew for sure Danny had sent the roses but they'd never know if he had been the anonymous shooter that day on the hill.

Seth's theory was that Danny assumed the money had been found by his aunt and was long gone. Her finding the cash would explain how Eric had started his business. He doubted that Danny knew about his brother cleaning out his 401K. So there had been no point going to get it, which was why he was cooking meth for profit.

Brittany was facing a slew of charges and Presley couldn't help feeling sorry for the woman. A little. The woman was clearly troubled if she'd been that desperate. Hopefully she would get her life back under control at some point in the future.

And Eric had settled into witness protection quite well from what Evan had told them, although at some point he'd have to testify, but that could be years away.

"Can I help, babe?"

Hands on her hips, she gave him a disgusted look as she fussed with her ponytail. Her hair was practically standing straight up. "You bet you can. Where have you been, anyway? You said you were going to stop by an hour ago."

Seth waded into the boxes packed in the small space. "I had to go out on a call. Just what am I looking for, by the way?"

"Paper cups. All sizes. We need to restock under the counter. Are you hungry? Eliza made lemon cookies. They're still warm."

Seth hefted a large box onto his shoulder, making it look easy. "I could eat. Why don't you make us a couple of coffees and take a little break with me before I have to get back to the station?"

Presley took a deep breath and gathered all of her courage. She'd been keeping this secret for almost four and half hours and that was way too long for her. This wasn't the most opportune moment or place to break the news but she simply couldn't keep it to herself any longer.

"I can make you some coffee but I won't be drinking any for about the next eight months or so."

Her handsome husband froze, his entire body motionless. His eyes widened slightly and then he seemed to start breathing again as he carefully placed the box back down on the floor.

"I'm not sure what you mean."

Seth knew exactly what she was talking about.

"Are you sure? Because you should know." She approached him slowly. almost scared he'd bolt. She placed a hand on his chest and she could feel his heart racing under her palm. Exactly like her own. "I'm pregnant."

He blinked. Once. Twice. Three times. Then he swallowed hard, his throat bobbing.

"Pregnant. Are you sure?"

She nodded, letting him absorb the news in his own time. "I took a test this morning before I dropped the kids at your parents'. Do you need to sit down? You're not going to ask me how it happened, are you?"

He shook his head but he still looked dazed as if hit by a wooden beam, smack across the forehead.

"No, I mean…we both knew this was a possibility because we weren't taking any precautions in Vegas."

That made her giggle. "I guess what happens there doesn't always stay there."

Rubbing the back of his neck, she could see a smile beginning to bloom on his face. Her precious Seth was happy. She was, too. There were a million practical reasons not to have another baby. None of them mattered. She already loved this child.

"A baby."

The way he said it made her heart flutter against her ribs. His tone was hushed, almost reverent.

"A baby," she repeated. "I'm really happy. Are you okay with it?"

Grinning, he grabbed her, lifting her up and spinning her around until she yelped for mercy.

"Stop or you'll have me puking up my breakfast. You know how sick I was with Ben and Lulu."

As quickly as it had come his smile was gone, replaced with a sober expression. "Honey, maybe I should—"

Shaking her head, Presley pressed her hand over Seth's mouth. They'd had this conversation several times since that day a gun had been pointed at her in the barn. "Don't even finish that sentence. You are a wonderful lawman and this town needs you."

He pried her fingers away from his lips. "You need me too, and so do the kids. Maybe I should quit—"

"Stop. Stop. Stop." She pressed her hands to her ears. "I'm not listening, Seth Reilly."

"Jesus, you are so frustrating, woman. I am trying to be noble here."

"Well, quit it. It's annoying." She clasped her hands together in mock delight. "Oh goody, the mood swings have shown up. You are going to have so much fun, my darling husband."

But Seth wasn't laughing. His eyes were bright and his hands were shaking as he pulled her close. If he was going to get emotional, then dammit, so was she. Didn't he remember that she could cry at the drop of a hat when she was pregnant? Here come the waterworks.

"I just don't think you realize how much I love you, honey." He lifted her feet off of the ground again. "Three. We're going to have three children. Do you think it will be a boy or a girl? Do you have a preference? Shit, we need to get that addition built onto the house. And we gave away all the baby stuff, we'll need to do some shopping. Cribs, and a new rocking chair–"

"Yes, we have lots to do," Presley said, stopping his flow of words. He liked his control and pregnancy wasn't exactly something that cooperated but she'd let him do what he needed to make him feel better. "But one thing at a time. What's the first thing you should do, Seth Reilly, when your wife tells you she's pregnant?"

Now she was a blubbering mess. It was all his fault.

She was such a sucker for that sexy smile that never ceased to brighten her day. She was going to love this man forever. She couldn't wait to grow old by his side. She couldn't wait to have another baby that looked just like him.

"Kiss you and tell you I love you. I guess I got a little carried away. I love you, honey."

"I love you too. Now kiss me. You're going to be a daddy again."

*I hope you enjoyed Seth and Presley's second happily ever after! Thank you for reading Vengeful Justice!*

**Don't miss a thing!**
**Sign up to be notified of Olivia's new releases:**
oliviajaymesoptin.instapage.com

# About the Author

Olivia Jaymes is a wife, mother, lover of sexy romance, and caffeine addict. She lives with her husband and son in central Florida and spends her days with handsome alpha males and spunky heroines.

She is currently working on a new contemporary romance series – The Hollywood Showmance Chronicles in addition to the ongoing Danger Incorporated series and the Cowboy Justice Association series.

Visit Olivia Jaymes at
www.OliviaJaymes.com

# Other Titles by Olivia Jaymes

## Danger Incorporated

Damsel In Danger
Hiding From Danger
Discarded Heart Novella
Indecent Danger
Embracing Danger
Danger In The Night
Reunited With Danger

## Cowboy Justice Association

Cowboy Command
Justice Healed
Cowboy Truth
Cowboy Famous
Cowboy Cool
Imperfect Justice
The Deputies
Justice Inked
Justice Reborn
Vengeful Justice

## Military Moguls

Champagne and Bullets
Diamonds and Revolvers
Caviar and Covert Ops
Emeralds, Rubies, and Camouflage

## Midnight Blue Beach

Wicked After Midnight
Midnight Of No Return
Kiss Midnight Goodbye

## The Hollywood Showmance Chronicles

A Kiss For the Cameras
Swinging From A Star

Made in the USA
Columbia, SC
10 December 2020

27094568R00150